Y

Sco

4

50 Shared texts

Photocopiable texts for shared reading

- Fiction, non-fiction and poetry
- Annotated versions
- Discussion prompts

Wendy Jolliffe,
Claire Head & David Waugh

Credits

Authors
Wendy Jolliffe,
Claire Head and
David Waugh

Series Consultants
Fiona Collins and
Alison Kelly

Editor
Clare Gallaher

Assistant Editor
Roanne Charles

Illustrations
Terry Burton

Series Designer
Anna Oliwa

Designer
Anna Oliwa

Designed using Adobe InDesign

Published by Scholastic Ltd
Villiers House
Clarendon Avenue
Leamington Spa
Warwickshire CV32 5PR

www.scholastic.co.uk

Printed by Bell and Bain Ltd, Glasgow

3 4 5 6 7 8 9   5 6 7 8 9 0 1 2 3

British Library Cataloguing-in-Publication Data
A catalogue record for this book is available from the British Library.

ISBN 0-439-98479-3

Contents

Term 2 *continued*

Term 3

N *Teacher's notes* P *Photocopiable*

Introduction

In *50 Shared texts* you will find a range of texts for use in shared reading. In recent years shared text work has become the focal point of daily literacy work, and the success of such shared work is clearly linked to the quality and choice of text. Better understanding of children's reading and writing development has led to the realisation that a greater range of text types, or genres, is needed to enrich children's literacy development. For the busy classroom teacher, seeking out such a range of quality texts can be too time-consuming, which is why appropriate texts have been provided in this book.

Shared reading

Shared reading is at the heart of the activities in this book and is a cornerstone of the National Literacy Strategy, which states that through shared reading children *begin to recognise important characteristics of a variety of written texts, often linked to style and voice.*

First developed in New Zealand by Don Holdaway, shared reading has been a significant literacy routine for children since the 1980s. Holdaway's research and pioneering work in schools brought the benefits of sharing enlarged texts or Big Books to teachers' attention. From his observations of very young children attending to bedtime stories on a one-to-one basis he realised that a similar intimacy with print could be offered through sharing an enlarged text with a group or class of children. He showed how engagement with Big Books can teach children about the characteristics of different text types, their organisation and distinguishing features, as well as the finer details of print. For example, depending on the teacher's focus, an enlarged recipe could be used at text level to model the way a piece of instructional writing is structured, at sentence level to look at the use of imperative verbs or at word level to focus on a particular phoneme. In relation to literature, the meaning of a poem can be explored at text level, the poet's choice of verbs at sentence level and the rhyming pattern at word level. So, shared reading not only encourages the class to share the actual reading aloud of a text but also enables the teacher to discuss certain language features and support the children in both comprehending and responding to the text.

With younger children, shared reading involves following the text with a pointer to highlight key early concepts of print such as directionality and one-to-one correspondence. With such concepts securely in place, a rather different technique is needed for older children where the focus shifts more to understanding and responding to the text as well as discussing vocabulary and linguistic features. For all children, often the talk surrounding the reading is as important as the reading itself.

Finding the right quality texts for shared reading that will engage and interest the children, as well as meeting the many NLS objectives, can be a difficult task. Once a text is found, you need to identify salient features at word, sentence and text level.

Shared reading is also the springboard for shared writing, guided reading/writing and independent work. Both guided reading and writing provide opportunities for you to guide, support, model and comment on children's response to a text. Activities may involve reading aloud, role-play, performance or writing for a particular purpose. Independent activities may mirror these but need to be clearly structured to enable the children to work independently.

About this book

The texts in this book are organised term by term, following the NLS framework, so there are examples of fiction, poetry, plays and non-fiction.

For each text, both a blank and annotated version are provided. The former is for use with children and can either be enlarged or projected on an overhead projector; the latter is for teacher information and identifies the features of the text and links with NLS objectives.

Background
Background information is provided for each text. This will contextualise the extract, fill in any necessary details and give facts about its author as relevant. Information on themes, technical features or other related texts might also feature here.

Shared reading and discussing the text
This section offers guidance on ways of managing discussion around the text, as well as ways of organising the shared reading. Depending on the age of the children, and demands of the text, different strategies for working with the whole class on the text are given, as well as ways of triggering the children's responses. These include structured discussion suggestions, ideas for role-play, and performance techniques.

Activities
Building on the reading and discussion, this section suggests activities for both whole-class work and guided or independent group work. There are ideas for further textual analysis, sometimes involving shared writing. As in the previous section, talk is pivotal in developing the children's understanding.

Extension/further reading
Suggestions for taking activities into a broader context and ideas for linked reading are also provided, where appropriate. Reading may include books of the same genre, or texts that share the theme or the same author.

The texts
The choice of texts has been driven by the need to ensure that these are quality texts both in content and language. It is hoped that among the selection you will find a mixture of authors and texts, both familiar and new. Whole texts have been provided as far as possible so that children have the satisfaction of reading and appreciating a coherent and complete piece of writing.

Longer texts, such as novels, also need to feature in older children's reading, and sometimes more than one extract from the same carefully chosen novel has been included. Bearing in mind that children should experience as much of the novel as they can, it is recommended that you use the background notes to fill the children in on plot detail, and that you read the story to them or have copies, including a taped version, available for their own reading or listening. Other slots in the curriculum can be used for such reading: private reading, homework, independent group work or story time.

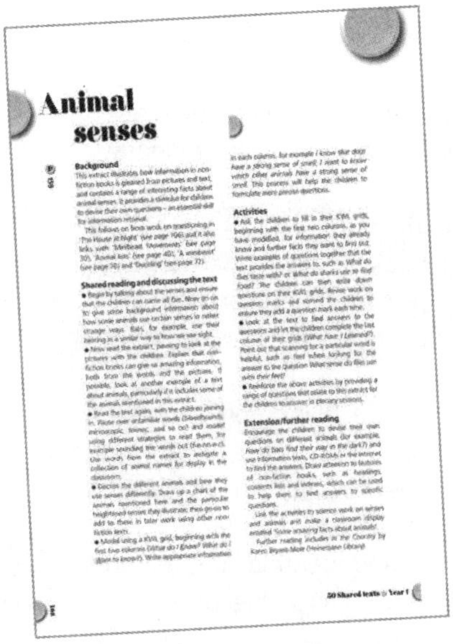

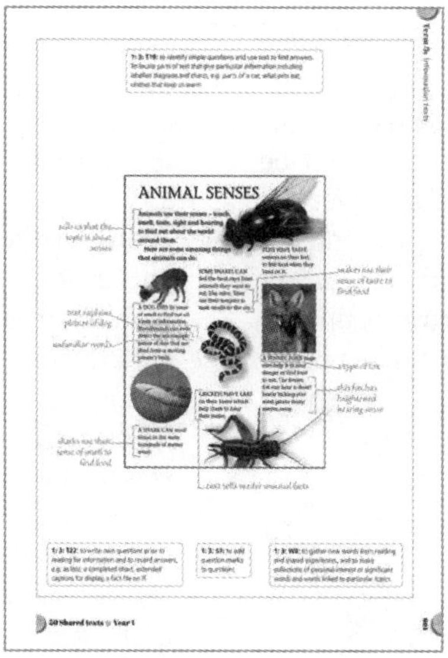

Range and objectives

Year 1 Term 1

Range	Text	NLS references
Stories with familiar settings	**'The Tiger who came to tea'** from *The Tiger who came to tea* by Judith Kerr (Picture Lions)	W12, S2, S3, T5 T10
	'Lucy's Picture' from *Lucy's Picture* by Nicola Moon (Orchard Books)	S2, S5, T5, T15
	'Tell Me What It's Like to Be Big' from *Tell Me What It's Like to Be Big* by Joyce Dunbar (Corgi Juvenile)	T5, T9
	'What Can I Write? Rosie Writes Again' from *What Can I Write? Rosie Writes Again* by Martina Selway (Red Fox)	S9, T4, T9
	'Where Are You, Blue Kangaroo?' from *Where Are You, Blue Kangaroo?* by Emma Chichester Clark (Collins)	S5, T5, T6, T7, T9
Stories and rhymes with predictable and repetitive patterns	**'It's the Bear!'** from *It's the Bear!* by Jez Alborough (Walker Books)	W1, S3, T1, T6, T10, T15
	'Summer Rain' by Jean Kenward from *Secrets* compiled by Judith Nicholls in the *All Aboard* series (Ginn)	W1, T4, T6, T10
	'Follow My Leader!' from *Follow My Leader!* by Emma Chichester Clark (Picture Lions)	S3, T1, T3, T10
	'Who Likes Cornflakes?' by Wes Magee from *Hop to the Sky* compiled by Brian Moses in the *All Aboard* series (Ginn)	W1, W3, T1, T11
	'Seeds' by Hilda I Rostron from *Seed Poems* compiled by John Foster (Oxford University Press)	S3, T6, T7, T10
	'Minibeast Movements' by Tony Mitton from *Secrets* compiled by Judith Nicholls in the *All Aboard* series (Ginn)	W3, T6, T10
	'What's in Your Pocket, Lucy Locket?' from *What's in Your Pocket, Lucy Locket?* by Paul and Emma Rogers (Bodley Head)	W10, S4, T7, T10, T14
Signs; lists; instructions	**'Rules for the cloakroom'** by David Waugh	W3, W4, W5, W6, W8, T13, T16
Labels; captions	**'Plan of a school'** by David Waugh	W8, W12, T12
Labels	**'Labelled drawers'** by David Waugh	W2, W8, W12, T12, T16
Lists	**'Animal lists'** by David Waugh	W1, W3, W4, W5, W6, W8, T15
	'Make a list' by David Waugh	W9, W10, T15

Year 1 Term 2

Range	Text	NLS references
Traditional stories and rhymes	**'Little Red Riding Hood'** from *Little Red Riding Hood* retold by Tony Ross (Andersen Press)	W10, S2, S3, T4
	'The Frog Prince' retold by Stephen Corrin in *Stories for Six-year-olds* edited by Sara and Stephen Corrin (Puffin)	W6, S2, S3, T6, T8
	'The Three Wishes' (extract 1) retold by David Waugh	W10, S2, S3, T7, T8, T16
	'The Three Wishes' (extract 2) retold by David Waugh	W2, S2, T4, T9, T14
	'The Tortoise and the Hare' retold by David Waugh	S2, S6, T4, T8
	'The Three Little Pigs' by Marian Swinger from *The Works* chosen by Paul Cookson (Macmillan Children's Books)	W3, S3, T4, T11, T14
Poems with familiar, predictable and patterned language	**'Half a Moon and One Whole Star'** from *Half a Moon and One Whole Star* by Crescent Dragonwagon (Aladdin)	W6, W9, T12, T13
	'Weather' by Eve Merriam from *Time for a Rhyme* chosen by Fiona Waters (Orion Children's Books)	W1, W2, W3, W7, S3, T1, T11, T13
Plays	**'Whose is it?'** by Charles Thomson from *Another First Poetry Book* compiled by John Foster (Oxford University Press)	W6, W9, T7, T9
Information books, including non-chronological reports	**'From seed to sunflower'** from *From Seed to Sunflower* by Dr Gerald Legg in the *Lifecycles* series (Franklin Watts)	T17, T18, T22
	'Keeping fit' from *Keeping Fit* by Paul Bennett in the *Body Works* series (Belitha Press)	W3, W10, T17, T22, T24, T25
	'Hearing' from *Hearing* by Mandy Suhr in *The Senses* series (Wayland)	T17, T18, T25
	'Weather: rain' by Jillian Powell from *Rain and Us* in the *Weather* series (Belitha Press)	T19, T22, T23, T25
	'A minibeast' from The Natural History Museum's *Insects and Other Minibeasts* by Barbara Taylor in the *Animal Close-ups* series (Oxford University Press)	T17, T18, T21, T22, T25
	'Duckling' from *Baby Animals* by Angela Royston in the *Eye Openers* series (Dorling Kindersley)	T17, T22, T24, T25
	'Healthy eating' by Claire Head	T17, T22, T25

Year 1 Term 3

Range	Text	NLS references
Stories about fantasy worlds	**'UFO Diary'** from *UFO Diary* by Satoshi Kitamura (Red Fox)	W8, S6, T7
	'Through the Magic Mirror' from *Through the Magic Mirror* by Anthony Browne (Walker Books)	W1, W7, T8, T14
	'Falling Angels' from *Falling Angels* by Colin Thompson (Red Fox)	W1, T4, T8
	'The Brave Little Grork' from *The Brave Little Grork* by Kathryn Cave (Hodder Children's Books)	W6, T5, T14
Poems with patterned and predictable structures	**'Porwigles'** by Julie Holder from *A First Poetry Book* compiled by John Foster (Oxford University Press)	W5, W6, S3, T1, T2, T11
	'Here is the Nose' by Clyde Watson from *Twinkle Twinkle Chocolate Bar* compiled by John Foster (Oxford University Press)	S4, T10, T16
	'There Was an Old Woman' from *Collected Poems for Children* by Charles Causley (Macmillan Children's Books)	W1, T10, T16
	'When the Wind Blows' by John Foster from *Twinkle Twinkle Chocolate Bar* compiled by John Foster (Oxford University Press)	W5, W8, S3, T9, T15, T16
	'The March Wind' from *Time for a Rhyme* chosen by Fiona Waters (Orion Children's Books)	W1, T9, T11, T16
	'The Sound of the Wind' by Christina Rossetti from *Time for a Rhyme* chosen by Fiona Waters (Orion Children's Books)	S7, T9, T11, T16
Stories with patterned and predictable structures	**'When I'm Big'** from 'When I'm Big' by Debi Gliori from *The Walker Treasury of Goodnight Stories* (Walker Books)	S2, T6, T14
	'But Martin!' from *But Martin!* by June Counsel (Picture Corgi)	W6, S5, T10, T13
Information texts including recounts	**'A first night away'** by Wendy Jolliffe	W6, T18, T20
	'How my body has changed' by Wendy Jolliffe	W7, T18, T20
	'I came to Britain from Jamaica' from *I Came to Britain from Jamaica* by Valerie Fawcett in the *Oxford Reading Tree Fact Finders* series (Oxford University Press)	W7, T18, T20
Information texts	**'The House at Night'** from *Inside My House* by Stephen Webster (Red Fox)	S7, T17, T22
	'Animal senses' by Wendy Jolliffe, based on an extract from *Children's Illustrated Encyclopedia* (Dorling Kindersley)	W8, S7, T19, T22

The Tiger who came to tea by Judith Kerr

P 110

Background

This extract is from a well-known first book by Judith Kerr. Sophie and her mother have been having their tea; the doorbell has rung and they have been speculating about who might be at the door. After this extract, the tiger goes on to eat and drink everything in Sophie's house.

Although this story has a familiar setting, children will particularly enjoy the fantastic elements of it, such as the tiger drinking all the water in the tap and the family buying tiger food in case the tiger visits again. These parts of the story can provoke discussion and lead to debate about what is possible and impossible. Antonia Fraser is quoted on the back cover; when the story was first published in 1968, she said that it would cause children to 'scream with delicious pleasure at the dangerous naughtiness of the notion'.

Shared reading and discussing the text

- Tell the children the story so far or, if you have a copy of the book, read the first three pages of the story to the children before showing them the text. Ask them if they already know the story and if anyone can remember who is at the door.
- Read the extract and ask the children what they would do if a tiger came to their houses and asked to be invited in for tea.
- Look at some of the unfamiliar words in the text, all of which are phonically regular, and show the children how they are made up of different phonemes, for example, *furry, stripy, excuse, hungry.*
- Talk with the children about the ways in which we can use the grammar of a sentence to decipher new or unfamiliar words. Do this in a practical way by re-reading the extract with some of the unfamiliar words which have been discussed covered up. Pause when a covered word is encountered, and read to the end of the sentence before returning to the covered word and asking what it might be.
- Look at the question which is the tiger's second sentence. Read the sentence to the children with appropriate expression for a question and ask them if they know which punctuation mark indicates that the sentence is a question. Although question marks are not introduced formally until term 3, children will meet them frequently in shared and independent reading, and some will already be aware of their function.

Activities

- Provide the children with some incomplete sentences related to the story and ask them to choose from a selection of words (*hungry, mummy, tea, door*) to complete them. For example:

  Sophie opened the ____.
  The tiger said he was very ____.
  The tiger asked if he could come to ____.
  Sophie's ____ said the tiger could come to tea.

- Ask the children to draw a familiar setting and include an animal in the picture which would not usually be seen in such a setting, for example an elephant in the classroom.
- In guided reading, focus on decoding words using awareness of grammar.

Extension/further reading

If you have a copy of the book, read the whole story to the children and ask them to tell you some of the things in it which could not happen in real life (such as a talking tiger and a tiger sitting at a table). Ask them to compare the themes in this fantasy with those in any other stories they know in which unlikely or impossible things happen.

Not Now, Bernard by David McKee (Red Fox), *Clever Polly and the Stupid Wolf* by Catherine Storr (Puffin) and *Suddenly!* by Colin McNaughton (Picture Lions) all feature monsters or animals doing things out of the ordinary. More able children could write their own stories, some in guided writing, in which animals talk and behave in unusual ways.

1: 1: T5: to describe story settings and incidents and relate them to own experience and that of others

1: 1: T10: to use rhymes and patterned stories as models for their own writing

The Tiger who came to tea

Sophie opened the door, and there was a big, furry, stripy tiger.
The tiger said, "Excuse me, but I'm very hungry. Do you think I could have tea with you?"
Sophie's mummy said, "Of course, come in."

title

story setting

adjectives to describe the tiger

new or unfamiliar words

grammatical awareness can be used to determine expression for these sentences

question mark affects the way sentence is read

grammar of sentence can be used to decipher this word

1: 1: S2: to use awareness of the grammar of a sentence to decipher new or unfamiliar words, e.g. predict text from the grammar, read on, leave a gap and re-read

1: 1: S3: to draw on grammatical awareness, to read with appropriate expression and intonation, e.g. in reading to others, or to dolls, puppets

1: 1: W12: to gather new words from reading and shared experiences, and to make collections of personal interest or significant words and words linked to particular topics

Lucy's Picture by Nicola Moon

P 111

Background

It is an ordinary day at school and Lucy's teacher has asked the children if they would like to paint a picture. Lucy looks at the bright-coloured paints but decides to use collage materials to make a special picture for her grandpa. As the story unfolds, we follow Lucy as she becomes absorbed in finding different materials and textures to use in her picture. The description is so detailed that readers begin to see the picture in their heads. It is only at the end of the story, when Lucy presents the finished picture to her Grandpa, that we discover he is blind.

In this extract, which offers a more challenging read, children will be able to relate to the incidents and characters in the familiar school setting. The setting allows the author to introduce some complex ideas that children can be invited to think about. The rich text, the characters' actions and the dialogue bring the story to life and build emotional ties.

Shared reading and discussing the text

- Before reading the extract, explain the setting for this story. Explain the task Lucy's teacher has set the class. Read the extract and ask the children who Lucy is making her picture for.
- Ask the children to look for clues in the text that give us information about Lucy's grandpa, for example he likes blue flowers because they smell nice. Ask the children to predict whether Grandpa will like the picture.
- During shared reading, pause to highlight the way that the author engages our senses to help us interact with the story. Look for examples of this in the text, such as *soft, green velvet into curvy mounds*.
- Read through the extract again and encourage the children to suggest adjectives that could be inserted before nouns in the text, such as *long, thin twigs; smooth, green leaves*.
- Ask the children to identify capital letters in the story and to explain why they have been used. (For a new sentence and for names.)

Activities

- Provide a feely bag and ask each child in the group to put his or her hand in it and describe the feel of the object. Scribe the list of adjectives generated on the board. The children must try to guess the mystery object. Once they have become more experienced at this game, encourage them to write clues for an object and then ask a partner to guess what it is. Clues/descriptions should be related to the senses, for example *it feels... it smells... it makes a ____ sound when you ____ it.* Clues can also be given regarding the purpose of the object, for example *you can use it to...*
- Another game using the adjectives generated could involve children in matching objects to the most appropriate adjective (written on large cards). This could form the basis of an interactive display, for example *feather = fluffy.*
- Invite the children to make their own collage pictures (a gardens theme would tie in with the story and the vocabulary discussed). Once completed, the children could ask a friend to feel their picture and to describe it with his or her eyes closed. As a conclusion, ask the children to list all the materials they used in their collage picture. This list could be displayed next to their work, for example *soft wool; shiny blue paper.*

Extension/further reading

If you have a copy of the book, sequence the events in Lucy's whole school day and follow this by asking the children to write a recount of their own school day. Encourage each child to focus on his or her favourite part of the day. The recounts can then be sequenced in chronological order. It would be useful to link this work with telling the time.

Find out about Louis Braille and his work. This could be introduced via guided reading.

Relevant books include *Louis Braille* by Tessa Potter, *Helen Keller* by Harriet Castor (Franklin Watts) and *Cleversticks* by Bernard Ashley (Picture Lions).

1: 1: T5: to describe story settings and incidents and relate them to own experiences and that of others

1: 1: T15: to make simple lists for planning, reminding, etc.

Lucy's Picture

Lucy started her picture. She cut some soft green velvet into curvy mounds, like hills, and stuck them on the paper. She made a lake out of blue shiny stuff, and put it in between the hills. Then she found some flowery dress material.

"Grandpa has flowers like this in his garden," Lucy told Mrs Kelly. "He likes the blue ones best because they have the nicest smell." She cut round the flowers and stuck them in little clumps along the edge of the lake.

At playtime Lucy was too busy to play. Instead she collected twigs and leaves and then she found two small feathers! She filled her empty juice cup with sand from the sandpit. At last it was time to go inside.

Now Lucy was very excited about Grandpa's picture. She made him a tree out of the twigs and the leaves, and stuck the feathers on the end of a branch. Then she spread some glue in a long winding band over the hills, and scattered sand over the glue to make a path.

familiar school setting

capital letters for names

author's descriptions appeal to our senses – we can imagine how things look, smell, feel, sound

adjectives 'long, thin' could be added

rich text that uses adjectives and dialogue to paint a vivid picture

adjectives 'smooth, green' could be added

challenging vocabulary

1: 1: S2: to use awareness of the grammar of a sentence to decipher new or unfamiliar words, e.g. predict text from the grammar, read on, leave a gap and re-read

1: 1: S5: to recognise full stops and capital letters when reading, and name them correctly

Tell Me What It's Like to Be Big

by Joyce Dunbar

P 112

Background

Joyce Dunbar's story about an endearing 'bunny' family is infused with warmth and a gentle sense of humour. Its homely setting, beautiful illustrations and familiar themes ensure young readers will be able to relate events to their own experiences. The two main characters, little Willa and her older brother Willoughby, are especially lovable.

The story in this book unfolds as the reader listens to a conversation between the two siblings about what it is like to be grown-up. Willa faces a problem familiar to all young children; she is not 'big' enough yet to do some things by herself. Luckily for Willa, big brother Willoughby is on hand to help her out, even when that means he is woken up very early in the morning to reach the cornflakes for her.

The repetitive phrases used in the simple exchanges between the two siblings make this story one that children will want to re-enact, allowing their own concerns and frustrations about growing up to surface.

Shared reading and discussing the text

- Before reading the extract, talk about the two main characters, Willa and Willoughby, and explain the background to the conversation you are about to share with the class. Encourage the children to talk about their own younger and older brothers and sisters. What sorts of things do they or their family help each other with?
- Tell the children that you are going to read the text, which is a conversation between the two little bunnies, and that you are going to use a different type of voice for each bunny. Can the children engage with the text by spotting when Willa or Willoughby is talking? After reading part of the extract, pause to talk about the layout of the text on the page and the use of punctuation to help the reader. How do we know when Willa has asked a question? Identify question marks, question words and the word *asked* which is sometimes used instead of *said*.
- Re-read the extract and ask the children to join in, reading the text in an expressive voice. Choose individuals to demonstrate how to read different parts of the dialogue.
- Focus on the way that Willa repeats the question *'Will I?'* and the use of the conversational style, which makes the extract sound like a real conversation.
- Ask the children to describe how they feel about the characters after reading this conversation. Explain that authors often include conversations between characters in stories to bring the characters to life. This helps the reader to understand a character's personality and that makes it easier to predict what characters might do in different situations.
- After shared reading, ask the children to talk about things they will be able to do when *they* are older. Use examples from the extract as a starting point.

Activities

- Write character descriptions of Willa and Willoughby. What do we know about these two characters based on evidence presented in the story? (For example, *Willoughby can turn on the shower by himself and Willoughby is kind to his sister.*) This could be modelled through shared writing.
- During guided work, ask the children to rehearse orally and then write a sentence about something they can do independently, for example *I can make my own bed.* This could be initiated in circle time when each child could be encouraged to complete a sentence starting with *I can… (by myself).*
- During subsequent lessons, transfer these sentences onto strips of card so that they can be cut up for children to reassemble. Encourage the children to check that the sentences make sense and begin with a capital letter and end with a full stop. Once this task is completed, children in the group can guess who the author of each sentence is. The next step could involve turning these statements into questions, for example *Can you make your own bed?*

1: 1: T5: to describe story settings and incidents and relate them to own experiences and that of others

Tell Me What It's Like to Be Big

"Tell me what it's like to be big," said Willa.
"You can do lots of things," said Willoughby.
"What things?"
"You'll be able to reach the lamp by yourself when you're big," said Willoughby.
"Will I?" said Willa.
"Oh yes," said Willoughby. "And when you're really big, nearly as big as I'll be, you might be able to reach the moon in a rocket!"
"What else will I do when I'm big?" asked Willa.
"You'll be able to stand in the shower like me and turn it on by yourself," said Willoughby.
"Will I?" said Willa.
"You'll be able to reach for a towel and get dried by yourself," said Willoughby.
"Will I?" said Willa.
"And you'll be able to brush your own teeth without any help," said Willoughby.
"And will Spotty Ted brush his?" asked Willa.
"He hasn't got any teeth," said Willoughby.

new line for each new speaker

repeated use of question words

repetition of phrases

pattern broken when repetitive exchange ends in a comical way

tall, grown-up

main characters – names begin with capital letters

helps to identify questions

evidence about Willoughby

1: 1: T9: to write about events in personal experience linked to a variety of familiar incidents from stories

What Can I Write? Rosie Writes Again by Martina Selway

P 113

Background

This is Martina Selway's second story about Rosie, a young girl (approximately six years old) who we first meet through her postcards home in *Wish You Were Here*. This time Rosie is at school and her teacher has asked the class to write about the school holidays. Rosie insists she has nothing to say as she didn't do anything exciting in the holidays. However, each page in the book, which represents Rosie's workbook, reveals the comical everyday adventures she has had.

Shared reading and discussing the text

- Read the introductory paragraph to the children and discuss the setting, the main character, and her reason for writing. Ask the children to predict the sort of things Rosie might write about. What sort of things do the children do in their own school holidays?
- Read the recount of the first day. How do we know Rosie is the author?
- Talk about the use of *I* and *my* in the extract. Point out the features of a recount, for example the scene is set in the first sentence; events are recounted as they occur; the passage of time is signalled by a variety of connectives such as *first, afterwards*; it is written in the past tense; we learn about how the character felt; it ends with a closing statement.
- Place an acetate sheet over the text. Can the children identify the capital letters? Highlight these and talk about the use of capital letters at the start of names and new sentences.
- Read the text so that the children can hear Rosie's voice through the use of the first person and the way that she describes her feelings. Explain that it is important to include this sort of detail to bring the recount to life and to hold the reader's interest.
- Ask the children to predict what happened on day two of Rosie's holiday.

Activities

- Demonstrate to the children how to write a recount by modelling this on the board. First, verbally recount something about your weekend, for example a visit to the supermarket, garden centre, park, and so on. Think aloud as you are doing this in order to make the drafting process explicit to the children. It is useful to establish prompts at this stage that will help to organise the content:
  1. Set the scene. *On Saturday I went...*
  2. Recount events in the order that they happened. *First I checked I had my list and then...*
  3. Use connectives that signal time. *Next I... Afterwards I...*
  4. Describe/explain incidents that are important and try to make them interesting for the reader by explaining how you felt. *Suddenly, the basket tipped up and the eggs fell out. I was horrified. I thought they would be broken.*
  5. Finish with a closing statement commenting on events. *When I got home I told my friend all about it.*
- Read through your recount together with the children and check it makes sense. Ask the children to work in pairs to answer the following questions related to your recount: *who, when, what, how, why?*
- Create a writing frame based on this session to scaffold children's own attempts at writing a recount. This could be introduced during guided group work. Provide children with a word bank of temporal connectives, and remind them about verbs with *ed* past tense endings, for example *I visit<u>ed</u> the...*

Extension/further reading

Ask the children to work in pairs and read their recounts to each other. Each child must think of one question she wants to ask her partner to find out more about events outlined. Alternatively, children could record their recounts using a tape recorder.

Books for further reading include *Busy Places – Supermarket* and *A Day in the Life of a Farmer* by Carol Watson (Franklin Watts) and *Going to School* by Anne Civardi (Usborne).

1: 1: T9: to write about events in personal experience linked to a variety of familiar incidents from stories

1: 1: S9: to use a capital letter for the personal pronoun 'I' and for the start of a sentence

What Can I Write?
Rosie Writes Again

Rosie's teacher has asked the class to write a story about what they did in the holidays. Rosie can't think of a single thing. She hadn't been anywhere. She hadn't done anything.

She asked, "What can I write?"

Miss West said, "Come on, Rosie, just start!"

The first day of my holiday Mum was working.[1] [2]
I had to go to Mrs Benn's next door. I don't like Mrs Benn much and I didn't like what she cooked for lunch. It was horrible liver and onions and cabbage. I wouldn't eat it.
Mrs Benn said, "Children today don't know what's good for them."
She gave it to her cat Lilly and I had a cheese sandwich. Afterwards I played with Lilly while Mrs Benn was knitting. Lilly got the wool in a terrible mess!

When Mum came back to get me she promised we'd go to the Toy Museum next day.

introduction sets scene and introduces main character

page from Rosie's writing book – this is her first recount

verbs in past tense ('ed' ending)

use of capital letters for names and new sentences

connective that signals time

closing statement gives hint of next recount

reflects Rosie's feelings

1. scene setting in opening statement

2. events recounted in order

personal opinion to engage reader's sympathy

1: 1: T4: to read familiar, simple stories and poems independently, to point while reading and make correspondence between words said and read

Where Are You, Blue Kangaroo?

by Emma Chichester Clark

P 114

Background

Lily is easily distracted and often loses her precious toy, Blue Kangaroo. Luckily, lots of kind people are always on hand to help her find him – that is, until Blue Kangaroo decides to teach Lily a lesson one day. Happily, in the end the friends are reunited and decide that the best place for Blue Kangaroo to be is in a pouch attached to Lily.

This endearing story is Emma Chichester Clark's first tale about Lily and her beloved Blue Kangaroo and was shortlisted for the Kate Greenaway Medal. Children will identify with the familiar settings and themes in the story and will be able to relate to the main character and her feelings about her favourite toy.

Shared reading and discussing the text

- After reading the extract, talk about the first two simple sentences that introduce us to the main characters and explain who they are. Discuss the use of capital letters and the place of full stops.
- Draw attention to the question that is repeated in the extract: *'Where are you Blue Kangaroo?'* Ask the children to consider how Lily feels when she realises she has lost Blue Kangaroo. Relate this to the children's own experiences of losing favourite toys. Children could talk to a friend about a time when they lost something important to them.
- Read with the children the line: *And Blue Kangaroo waited for Lily to find him.* Help the children to see that this allows the reader to view events from another perspective – from Blue Kangaroo's point of view. (This is repeated throughout the book whenever Lily loses Blue Kangaroo.)
- Ask the children to consider how Blue Kangaroo is feeling when he knows Lily has forgotten him or lost him. Point out that sometimes the author tells us how characters are feeling, for example *she wasn't scared on the slide.*
- The author also chooses language very carefully to add layers of meaning and to bring the text to life. For example, a range of synonyms are used instead of the word *said,* such as *shrieked, asked* and *smiled.* Talk about the meaning of the word *shrieked* and ask the children to practise reading to a friend with the appropriate expression, *Lily suddenly shrieked, 'Where are you Blue Kangaroo?'*
- Discuss the use of dialogue in the text. Explain to the children that this helps us to empathise with characters (for example, Florence is worried that Lily might lose her toy and this shows the reader that Florence is kind and cares for Lily). The dialogue also helps to move the plot along (Aunt Jemima is also worried about Blue Kangaroo when she takes Lily out). The conversation between the characters can give the reader a hint of things to come, for example when Florence warns Lily, *'You must try to be more careful'* and Aunt Jemima encourages Lily to *'Hold tight to Blue Kangaroo.'*
- Ask the children to predict what will happen when Lily goes shopping with Aunt Jemima.

Activities

- Encourage the children to act out the story through role-play. To prepare for this, organise a session in which the children can interview Lily, Florence and Blue Kangaroo, as a hot-seating activity. You may need to model this by assuming one of the roles and answering children's questions as that character.
- Use the character interviews as a stimulus to create a word bank that can be used during shared writing. For example, model how to complete a 'lost' poster for the missing Blue Kangaroo. Children can then attempt this independently using a 'lost' poster writing frame and the word bank.

Extension/further reading

Ask the children to write their own story about a lost toy. They may like to read *Where's My Teddy?* by Jez Alborough, *This is the Bear and the Scary Night* by Sarah Hayes (Walker Books) and *Dogger* by Shirley Hughes (Red Fox).

1: 1: T5: to describe story settings and incidents and relate them to own experience and that of others

1: 1: T6: to recite stories and poems with predictable and repeating patterns, extemporising on patterns orally by substituting words and phrases, extending patterns, inventing patterns and playing with rhyme

Where Are You, Blue Kangaroo?

Blue Kangaroo belonged to Lily.
He was her very own kangaroo.
Sometimes Blue Kangaroo disappeared and Lily would say,
"Where are you, Blue Kangaroo?"
And Blue Kangaroo waited for Lily to find him.

One day, Lily's friend, Florence, took Lily to the park.
"Hold tight to Blue Kangaroo," said Florence.

Lily swung on the swings, and she wasn't scared on the slide.

"I love ice-cream!" said Lily...

...and Blue Kangaroo wondered if Lily had forgotten him.

As they were leaving, Lily suddenly shrieked, "Where are you, Blue Kangaroo?"
"Did you leave him on the slide?" asked Florence.

"Here he is!" smiled Lily.
"You must try to be more careful," said Florence.

The next Saturday, Lily's Aunt Jemima took Lily shopping.
"Hold tight to Blue Kangaroo," said Aunt Jemima.

capital letters for names

Lily's special toy – a toy that she loses sometimes

question repeated later

dialogue helps to move plot along and gives hint of things to come from new characters

familiar setting, and familiar experience for most children

Lily forgets Blue Kangaroo because she is distracted

allows us to view events from another perspective; we are told what Blue Kangaroo is thinking

used instead of 'said' – helps us to understand how to read the line in the voice of that character; also gives us clues about how character feels

author shows us that Florence and Aunt Jemima are kind, as they are worried about Blue Kangaroo getting lost

1: 1: T7: to re-enact stories in a variety of ways, e.g. through role-play, using dolls or puppets

1: 1: T9: to write about events in personal experience linked to a variety of familiar incidents from stories

1: 1: S5: to recognise full stops and capital letters when reading, and name them correctly

It's the Bear!

by Jez Alborough

P 115

Background

It's the Bear! is the second story that Jez Alborough has devoted to the characters of Eddy, his teddy and the giant bear that they encounter in the woods. In the first story, *Where's My Teddy?*, Eddy loses his toy bear, and a giant real-life bear finds it. This time, Mum also comes face to face with the hungry bear who sniffs out their picnic, and has to sacrifice her blueberry pie in order to escape with Eddy.

The exciting plot is carried along by the rhythmic language, the dialogue and the layout of the text. Children will delight in explaining the characters' emotions and the causes of incidents and problems as the story unfolds.

Shared reading and discussing the text

- Read the extract, then stop to allow the children to tell you anything they have noticed, for example that it rhymes. Identify the words that rhyme (for example, *dear/here; Freddy/ ready*) and ask the children how they spotted these.
- Read the extract again, pausing at appropriate points to encourage the children to predict and discuss the meaning of unfamiliar words, for example *gasped, hamper, clambered.*
- Ask the children to consider how particular events make individual characters feel, such as when Eddy sees the bear and realises his mother is not there: *SHE HAD GONE!* Ask the children to talk to a friend about a time when they have been scared and wished someone was there to help them.
- Explain to the children that the author is building up the suspense by making us anticipate the big scary bear. Ask the children to look at the last four lines of the extract and find out what we are told about the bear when we meet him, for example he is big, hungry, licking his lips and sniffing the air as he can smell food! (Point out the use of three dots close together – ellipsis – which also promotes excitement and an expectation of more to come.)
- Read the extract again, this time asking the children to join in. How does the author let us know how to make our voices sound when we are reading different parts of the text? Talk about the use of punctuation, particularly question marks to signal information is needed by a character and explanation marks to indicate strong feeling. Discuss the words printed in upper-case letters. These help to bring the text to life and encourage the reader to read with expression. Practise reading the dialogue using different voices.

Activities

- Ask the children to describe the giant bear. Model how to write a description, and create a word bank. Children can then work on their own descriptions.
- Make a list of things that the children would like to take on a picnic. Again this could be done initially as a shared writing exercise, with you demonstrating how to write a list. Encourage more able children to describe their picnic food, for example *crispy red apples.* Provide less able children with a picture of a picnic basket and ask them to draw their picnic things inside it; each child should then work with an adult to label his or her items.
- Create a role-play area where children can act out the story using props (ensure children are aware of the dangers of climbing inside a container and closing the lid). Independent role-play could be stimulated after conducting character interviews with the class following shared reading of the text.

Extension/further reading

Ask the children to predict what will happen when Eddy meets the bear. If you have a copy of the book you can read the ending and compare this to the children's ideas.

Once children know that the bear was harmless after all (he wanted to eat the blueberry pie, not Eddy), retell the story from the bear's point of view. This could be done orally or during shared writing.

1: 1: T15: to make simple lists for planning, reminding, etc.

1: 1: T1: to reinforce and apply their word-level skills through shared and guided reading

1: 1: S3: to draw on grammatical awareness, to read with appropriate expression and intonation, e.g. in reading to others, or to dolls, puppets

It's the Bear!

"A bear?" said Mum. "That's
silly, dear! R
We don't get great big bears
round here." R

"There's just you and me and
your teddy, Freddy.
Now let's all get the picnic
ready."

"We've got lettuce,
tomatoes,
creamy cheese spread, R
with hard-boiled eggs
and crusty brown bread. R
There's orange juice,
biscuits,
some crisps and –

OH MY!

I've forgotten to pack
the blueberry pie..."

"I'll pop back and get it,"
she said. "Won't be long."

"BUT MUM!"
gasped Eddy...

too late –
SHE HAD GONE!

He sat on the hamper
and tried not to cry,
then...

"I CAN SMELL FOOD!"
yelled a voice
from nearby.

"IT'S THE BEAR!"
cried Eddy.
"WHERE CAN I HIDE?"

Then he opened
the hamper and
clambered inside.

Out of the trees
stepped a big hungry bear,
licking his lips
and sniffing the air.

rhyming narrative text

author uses substitutes for 'said'

rhymes that sound the same but are spelled differently

capital letter for name

features of a list (commas to separate items)

use of direct speech moves plot along and helps us to relate to characters

we realise how the character feels

expectation of more to come

use of upper-case letters and exclamation mark brings the text to life and helps reader to read with expression

the big bear has been mentioned before we meet him, adding to suspense and anticipation

rhymes that sound the same and are spelled the same

unfamiliar/ unusual words

1: 1: W1: from YR, to practise and secure the ability to rhyme, and to relate this to spelling patterns through:
- exploring and playing with rhyming patterns
- generating rhyming strings, e.g. fat, hat, pat

1: 1: T6: to recite stories and poems with predictable and repeating patterns, extemporising on patterns orally by substituting words and phrases, extending patterns, inventing patterns and playing with rhyme

1: 1: T10: to use rhymes and patterned stories as models for their own writing

Summer Rain

by Jean Kenward

P 116

Background

'Summer Rain' is a delightful poem with a carefully constructed repetitive pattern in the style of 'Who Killed Cock Robin?'. Jean Kenward manages to evoke the feeling of the soft summer rain through subtle imagery as we peep into the world of three small creatures who sense the gentle raindrops fall.

The poem will provide you with the opportunity to focus on onset and rime in order to help children to extend rhyming patterns by analogy. It will also provide a stimulus and model for children's own writing.

Shared reading and discussing the text

- Before reading the poem, ask the children to look at the shape of the writing on the page. Does this give us a clue about the type of writing? Read the title together. Talk about how the poem is divided into three verses.
- Tell the children that you are going to read the whole poem to them and their job is to listen carefully and try to remember their favourite part. After reading, ask the children to talk about the poem with a friend. What is this poem about? Which part did they like/dislike? Ask a few pairs to feed back to the class.
- Ask the children to tell you how many creatures the poet describes. Place an acetate over the extract and highlight each creature. Explain that the poet uses the personal pronoun *I* to make us think that each creature is answering the question in the first line of each verse. For example, in the first verse the question *Who felt the rain begin?* is answered by the bat, *I, said the bat.*
- Read the poem again, with the children this time. Pause at the end of each verse to identify words and phrases that are repeated (for example, *Who...* and *I, said the...*). The repeated use of the question form at the start of each verse helps to define the type of rain and relate it to the senses, – that is, rain that is *felt* (verse 1), a shower that is *heard* (verse 2) and drops that are *sipped* (verse 3). These descriptions help us to imagine each creature's actions in its natural surroundings. Ask the children to talk about where they imagine each creature might be when the raindrops fall.
- The poet uses alliteration to help mimic the action of the little bird as it hops along – *Hurrying, hop-hop-hop.* Ask the children to read this line with you so that they can hear the stilted rhythm. Compare this to the sound of *Safe, in my secret skin* which has a slower, smoother pace as it describes the bat. Tell the children that you are going to read the last verse to them again and this time you want them to listen *and* to look at the text as you are reading and try to identify words that begin with the same letter sound (for example, *sipped/said; hurrying/hop; drank/drop*).
- Focus on verse 2, then verse 3, to highlight the rhyme scheme. Identify words that have the same rime but different onsets for example *f-all/w-all; dr-op/st-op/h-op.* Write these on the board and ask the children to think of more words with the same letter string.

Activities

- Prepare a set of rhyming words (taken from the poem) on cards and ask the children to work in pairs to sort the cards into rhyming sets, for example *drop/stop/hop; begin/skin/in.* Can they think of one more word that has the same *rime* and add it to the set?
- Give the children a copy of the poem and ask them to highlight words that contain specific phonemes, consonant clusters and digraphs. For example, if you give them *ai,* they should highlight *rain*; if you give them *dr* they should highlight *drop/drank*, and so on.
- Demonstrate to the children how to write a new verse using the structure and style of 'Summer Rain'. This could be done initially through shared writing in order to establish a frame to scaffold the children's writing. For example: question (*Who...?*), answer (*I, said the...*), description of creature (What does it look like, where is it, what does it do and how does it feel when the raindrops fall?); repetition of second line (*I, said the...*).

1: 1: T4: to read familiar, simple stories and poems independently, to point while reading and make correspondence between words said and read

1: 1: T6: to recite stories and poems with predictable and repeating patterns, extemporising on patterns orally by substituting words and phrases, extending patterns, inventing patterns and playing with rhyme

SUMMER RAIN

Who felt the rain begin?
I, said the bat.
Safe, in my secret skin,
darting now out, now in,
I felt the rain begin.
I, said the bat.

Who heard the shower fall?
I, said the snail.
High on the garden wall
I heard it splash and fall
summer rain over all.
I, said the snail.

Who sipped it, drop by drop?
I, said the bird.
I hoped it wouldn't stop!
Hurrying, hop-hop-hop
I drank it, drop by drop.
I, said the bird.

Jean Kenward

question at start of each verse (rain begins, becomes a shower, then is sipped in drops)

personal pronoun

unfamiliar vocabulary

these descriptions help us to imagine each creature's actions in its natural surroundings

in each verse, a different sense is referred to: touch in verse 1, hearing in verse 2, taste in verse 3

unfamiliar vocabulary

image of bat as a 'secret' creature, keeping to itself

repeated refrain in last line of each verse

a different creature in each verse

rhyming words that have same rime

words beginning with same letter (alliteration) help us to imagine the bird's quick movements

1: 1: T10: to use rhymes and patterned stories as models for their own writing

1: 1: W1: from YR, to practise and secure the ability to rhyme, and to relate this to spelling patterns through:
- exploring and playing with rhyming patterns
- generating rhyming strings, e.g. fat, hat, pat

Follow My Leader!

by Emma Chichester Clark

P 117

Background

This narrative verse adds a delightful poetic and comical twist to the well-known children's game 'Follow my leader'. The leader in this story is a little boy and he is being followed by animals who are his friends. The reader is swept along at an energetic pace as each verse gathers momentum until the characters playing the game meet a tiger – and the tiger wants to play too! The little boy needs to think of a way to trick the tiger and save his friends, so they continue to play follow my leader all the way home until everyone is safe indoors.

Shared reading and discussing the text

- Before reading the extract, draw the children's attention to the layout of the text and the repeated refrain *Follow my leader!* Explain that in this story a little boy has just started playing the game 'Follow my leader' with some of his animal friends in the woods. Ask the children if they know how to play this game. Involve a few children in a demonstration to help you explain the rules, for example one person (the leader) performs a series of actions and the other people playing the game have to follow the leader and copy his or her actions.
- Read the text and talk about the actions and movements that the characters copy, for example leaping and bounding, jumping and jiving. Discuss the pairs of verbs used in the second line of most of the verses.
- Read the text again and this time involve children in clapping along to the rhythm of each verse. Identifying syllables will help them to segment words when reading and writing.
- Ask the children to talk to a partner about their favourite part of the extract. Encourage the children to describe the physical features, for example *Over the stile, Round the corner,* as well as the action words.
- Draw the children's attention to the *ing* endings that rhyme and are repeated in each verse, for example *bounding, jumping* and *splashing*. Demonstrate how the spelling of some words changes when we add *ing*, for example *hop* – *hopping*. Ask the children to think of alternative movement words, and make a list of these on the board. Check the *ing* endings, for example *run* – *running* and *twirl* – *twirling*.
- Mask the prepositions (*over, up*, and so on) and re-read the extract, asking the children to suggest appropriate words. Discuss whether their choices make sense, then reveal the words the author chose.

Activities

- Ask the children to draw pictures to match each verse, visually representing events in the story. Use these pictures to retell the story in order. Make a story map and label significant physical features, for example *stile* and *hill*. Retell the story, using props/puppets/modelling clay figures and the map. Can the children retell the story in the correct sequence?
- Add new verses, using the same structure. Introduce this via modelling during shared writing and then encourage the children to write their own verses in guided and independent writing.
- Make a dice game based on the extract. On the sides of one dice write places, for example *up the hill*; on the sides of a second dice, write movement words, for example *splishing and splashing*. Tell the children to take it in turns to roll the dice (away from the group) and act out the movements. The rest of the group must guess what the two dice show by suggesting a sentence to describe the place and actions.

Extension/further reading

If you have a copy of the book, ask the children to talk about what they would do at the point in the story where the tiger asks to join the game. Encourage them to draw a storyboard and write simple sentences to explain their version. Compare this to the real ending.

We're Going on a Bear Hunt by Michael Rosen (Walker Books) and *The Gruffalo* by Julia Donaldson (Macmillan Children's Books) are similar in theme.

1: 1: T1: to reinforce and apply their word-level skills through shared and guided reading

1: 1: T3: to notice the difference between spoken and written forms through retelling known stories; compare oral versions with the written text

Follow My Leader!

Over the stile,
Leaping and bounding,
Follow my leader!

Up the hill,
Puffing and panting,
Follow my leader!

Round the corner,
Jumping and jiving,
Follow my leader!

Down the steps,
Bumping and thumping,
Follow my leader!

Across the stream,
Splishing and splashing,
Follow my leader!

Into the woods,
Shouting and roaring,
Follow my leader!

But wait…
Can you hear it?
Shhh! What's that noise?

RRROOOAAAR!

"I want to play,"
The tiger said, smiling.

Emma Chichester Clark

title makes us think of the game

repetition of this refrain at end of 1st 6 verses

action words that describe movements/sounds; 'ing' endings that create rhymes

prepositions

significant word describing how the tiger is feeling (this betrays his intentions)

in 1st 6 verses the number of syllables in 2nd and 3rd lines is the same (5 syllables)

physical features

question marks and exclamation mark alter pace and intonation

text designed for effect: volume and surprise

1: 1: T10: to use rhymes and patterned stories as models for their own writing

1: 1: S3: to draw on grammatical awareness, to read with appropriate expression and intonation, e.g. in reading to others, or to dolls, puppets

Who Likes Cornflakes? by Wes Magee

P 118

Background

'Who Likes Cornflakes?' is a humorous poem with a predictable, simple and repetitive pattern, which benefits from being read aloud. Children will enjoy the rhythmic qualities of the repeated question style and will appreciate the way that the layout of the words creates an interesting pattern on the page. This is an entertaining rhyme which will provide a useful stimulus for discussion and as a starting point for the children's own writing.

Shared reading and discussing the text

- Before reading the text, ask the children to look at an enlarged version and talk about the sort of writing it could be. Ask: *What clues tell us this is a poem?* Talk about its song-like quality and draw attention to the layout of the words on the page. Children may suggest it is a list or a set of questions, so it could be useful to compare how other texts are set out, visually, with this one. This poem almost sounds like a shopping list as the poet is checking which foods the family likes.
- Ask the children which words they can see/ read that are repeated on nearly every line of the poem (*Who* and *likes*). Talk about the change in layout (after the line *Who likes ice cream...*). This signals a break in the repetitive pattern and the lines narrow, dwindling away until the poem ends.
- Read the poem to the children and ask them to listen for further clues. Talk about words that sound the same (rhyme). Ask the children to read the poem with you so that they can *hear* the rhymes and *see* the text as you point to each word. Point out the way that some words sound the same but are spelled differently, for example *ch<u>eese</u>/p<u>eas</u>*.
- Ask a group of children to read the poem out loud, pausing after each question so that the rest of the class can put their hands up if the answer is *yes* to any of the questions. (At this point, remind the children that different people like and dislike different things and that we should respect their choices.)
- Talk about the use of question marks and question words (for example, *who, what, where, when, how, why*) and the way our voices might sound when we ask a question. Tell the children to look carefully at the text again and to identify another mark that helps the reader to interpret the text; talk about how the exclamation mark does this at the end of the poem.

Activities

- Play a circle game in which children take it in turns to complete the sentence *I like* _______, saying it aloud. Other children in the class should jump up and shout *'So do I'* if they like the same thing.
- Ask each child to write a sentence on a common theme, for example food – *I like bananas*, ensuring that their sentences begin with a capital letter and end with a full stop. They can then share their sentences in group sessions and turn them into questions, for example *Who likes bananas?* Remind the children about using capital letters and question marks. You could do this by cutting up simple sentences and questions, and asking the children to reassemble them and add the correct punctuation.
- Make a class or group poem using the children's questions based on the structure of the shared text. The children should be supported during shared or guided writing when composing the final exclamation that finishes the poem, for example *Who likes crackers for their snack? Teacher, Mum, my friend and Jack!*
- Encourage the children to write their own poem on a different theme, for example favourite animals, games or books.

Extension/further reading

The children may like to read *Ketchup on Your Cornflakes* by Nick Sharratt (Scholastic Press), *What's in Your Pocket, Lucy Locket?* by Paul and Emma Rogers (Bodley Head) and *Jack and Me and the Pizza* by Mick Gowar (Franklin Watts).

1: 1: T1: to reinforce and apply their word-level skills through shared and guided reading

1: 1: W1: from YR, to practise and secure the ability to rhyme, and to relate this to spelling patterns through:

- exploring and playing with rhyming patterns
- generating rhyming strings, e.g. *fat, hat, pat*

Who Likes Cornflakes?

Who likes cornflakes?
Who likes beans?
Who likes pizza?
Who likes greens?
Who likes apples?
Who likes cheese?
Who likes pudding?
Who likes peas?
Who likes ice cream
for their tea?
Grandma,
Mum,
and
Dad,
and
Me!

Wes Magee

predictable, repetitive pattern

layout of the poem emphasises repetition

question word

change in layout of poem signals a break in repeated pattern; lines shorten to become one word each, with shortest word at the end

almost like a shopping list

'ea'/'ee' spellings can make the same sound, for example 'beans', 'greens', but 'ea' makes a different sound in 'bread'

changes from a question to an exclamation

1: 1: W3: from YR to practise and secure the ability to hear initial and final phonemes in CVC words, e.g. fit, mat, pan

1: 1: T11: to make simple picture story books with sentences, modelling them on basic text conventions, e.g. cover, author's name, title, layout

Seeds

by Hilda I Rostron

P 119

Background

This poem is about different types of seeds and the ways in which they can be dispersed. It could be used to extend and enhance work begun in science lessons about seeds and plant growth. The poem's predictable, patterned structure conveys the energy and movement of the seeds through each rhyming couplet. Words have been chosen carefully to maintain the rhythm and appeal to the senses. There is also some subject-specific vocabulary to which children can be introduced. The poem provides opportunities to focus on blending consonant clusters and digraphs. It also offers a useful starting point for work on onset and rime.

Shared reading and discussing the text

- Before reading the poem, show the children a packet of seeds and briefly explain the instructions for planting. Talk about how different types of seeds find their way into the ground in different ways and do not need to rely on people planting them.
- Read the whole poem to the children so that they can appreciate the overall rhythm and the effect of the word choices. Explain that this is quite a difficult poem to read as you have to pronounce the sounds in each word carefully and the pace of the poem is quite fast. Invite the children to read the first two lines with you slowly, then once again more quickly.
- Identify the verbs that signify the actions of each seed, for example *twirl, float* and *burst.* Talk about the meanings of these words. Ask the children to pretend to be seeds and to act out each type of movement. Talk about how these movement words convey energy and are linked to different sorts of seeds, for example sycamore seeds twirl, dandelion seeds float.
- Read each couplet with the children and identify the words that rhyme. Provide the children with individual whiteboards and ask them to write down each rhyming pair and underline the part of each word that is the same, for example *ground, sound.* Ask the children to think of another word that rhymes with these. Write the words generated on the board and help the children to discriminate between onsets and rimes.
- Talk about how we need to blend some phonemes together when reading words, for example the consonant clusters *gr* and *spr.* Identify digraphs, for example *th, ch* (when two letters make one sound/phoneme).
- Discuss the meanings of unfamiliar words such as *thistledown, glossy* and *pods.* You could provide real examples or photographs of different types of seeds.

Activities

- Make a set of rhyming cards using the words from the poem, for example *cling* and *spring.* Play a rhyming pairs game with the children. Give each child a different card and ask each child in turn to say their word out loud. Continue until a rhyming pair of words is found. For each pair of rhyming words, encourage the children to think of another rhyming word with the same letter string, for example *ring* or *bring* (to go with *cling* and *spring*). This game could also be played using pairs of the same consonant cluster blends.
- In shared writing, model how to write a new verse for the poem. For example, *Seeds that fly* (verb/movement word) *and seeds that fall* (another action word beginning with the same phoneme). After looking at different types of seeds and making a list of adjectives and movement words, children could write their own sentences incorporating the vocabulary.
- During a PE lesson, ask the children to act out the movement of the seeds while you recite the poem (or the list of movement words generated during shared writing). Use music or percussion instruments to accompany the children's movements.

Extension/further reading

There are other poems about seeds in *Seed Poems* compiled by John Foster (OUP). *Let's Look at Nature* by Nicola Tuxworth (Lorenz Books) has a similar theme.

1: 1: T7: to re-enact stories in a variety of ways, e.g. through role-play, using dolls or puppets

1: 1: T10: to use rhymes and patterned stories as models for their own writing

Seeds

Seeds that twist and seeds that twirl
Seeds with wings which spin and whirl;

Seeds that float on thistledown
Seeds in coats of glossy brown;

Seeds that burst with popping sound
From their pods to reach the ground;

Seeds with hooks that clutch and cling
Seeds I plant for flowers next spring.

Hilda I Rostron

predictable, patterned structure

words chosen to show pace and rhythm of seeds falling

movement words convey energy and action

subject-specific terminology

rhyming couplets

consonant clusters blended when reading

appeals to senses

digraph

onset

rime

1: 1: S3: to draw on grammatical awareness, to read with appropriate expression and intonation, e.g. in reading to others, or to dolls, puppets

1: 1: T6: to recite stories and poems with predictable and repeating patterns, extemporising on patterns orally by substituting words and phrases, extending patterns, inventing patterns and playing with rhyme

Minibeast Movements

by Tony Mitton

P 120

Background

This is a simple repetitive poem that describes the movements of different minibeasts. The strong rhythm and the repeated first line in each verse makes it an ideal poem to read aloud and to use for extemporising on the pattern by replacing parts of the text with alternative words and phrases. The poem also makes use of alliteration, which provides a useful vehicle for work on hearing initial and final sounds in words. Links can be made to 'A minibeast' on page 70.

Shared reading and discussing the text

- Read the poem to the children. Talk about the choice of words the poet uses to describe the movements of the minibeasts, for example *stumbles, leaps, slides*, and ensure the children understand the vocabulary used, such as *clockwork* and *scuttles.*
- Now read it again, with the children joining in with expression. Look carefully at the rhythm of the poem and ask the children to clap the rhythm with you. Deliberately change the rhythm to help the children see the original version is much more fun to read, for example *clumsy, clockwork, slow* could be altered to *It is clumsy and moves like clockwork, slowly.*
- Look at the use of alliteration with the repeated use of *s*, such as *snail slides, smooth, steady, sure.* Ask the children to tell you what sound they can hear at the beginning of each word and if any words end in that sound (*slides*). Look at how the poet does the same in the last verse (*spider scuttles swiftly*).
- Highlight all the verbs, then read the poem with the verbs substituted for other verbs, such as the word *moves* each time. Which verbs sound best? Explain that poets choose words very carefully to give special effects.

Activities

- Work with a guided group to practise reading the poem while the children act out the movements of the different minibeasts – the beetle that moves like clockwork; the leaping grasshopper; the sliding snail; the scuttling spider. Demonstrate it to the whole class in a plenary session.
- Talk about the same words being repeated at the beginning of each verse and how poets often use this technique. Now change words and phrases to alter the poem, making sure that alliteration and a repeating pattern is retained, for example *This is the way the ladybird flutters, fanning flowers flat.* Provide the children with starter sentences, each beginning with *This is the way...* and a different minibeast each time. Discuss possible verbs (for example, *wriggles, flaps, slithers*) and provide a list to help them. Ask the children to work with a partner orally to rehearse alternative phrases. Provide individual whiteboards for them to make notes of words they choose.
- More able children can write verses (*This is the way...*) that each focus on a minibeast they have chosen themselves. Give less able children two sets of cards to match, one with pictures of minibeasts on them and one with words to describe how they move.
- Provide the children with individual copies of the poem and ask them to track for all the words that begin with *s* and underline them in red. They could find any words that end in *s* and underline them in an alternative colour. In a plenary session, use these lists to make further alliterative sentences.

Extension/further reading

Link this activity to science work on minibeasts. Research different types of minibeasts, providing firsthand experiences for the children by going on minibeast hunts or having a wormery or similar in the classroom. During close observation of different minibeasts, ask the children to describe how they move. They can then draw their minibeast and write a caption to say how it moves. This could be compiled into an alternative class poem.

Insects and other minibeasts by Barbara Taylor (OUP) shows close-up photographs of minibeasts.

1: 1: T6: to recite stories and poems with predictable and repeating patterns, extemporising on patterns orally by substituting words and phrases, extending patterns, inventing patterns and playing with rhyme

MINIBEAST MOVEMENTS

repeating pattern

This is the way
the beetle stumbles,
clumsy, clockwork, slow.

strong verb

alliteration

This is the way
the grasshopper leaps,
so, so, so!

This is the way
the snail slides,
smooth, steady, sure.

alliteration

similar to 1st verse – three adverbs

And this is the way
the spider scuttles
swiftly across the floor.

strong verb

alliteration

Tony Mitton

1: 1: T10: to use rhymes and patterned stories as models for their own writing

1: 1: W3: from YR to practise and secure the ability to hear initial and final phonemes in CVC words, e.g. *fit, mat, pan*

What's in Your Pocket, Lucy Locket?

by Paul and Emma Rogers

P 121

Background

The authors describe this story as 'a novelty book with pockets full of surprises'. The 'pockets' belong to a host of familiar characters from favourite nursery rhymes and traditional tales. The reader is introduced to these characters one by one as a search for a key is initiated at the start of the story. Who has the key to unlock the tower door and help Rapunzel? As usual, Lucy Locket has lost her pocket but her friends (including Pinocchio, Little Miss Muffet, Captain Hook and others) are asked to reveal the contents of their pockets in search of the key.

The narrative verse and the layout of the book invite the reader to explore the contents of each pocket. This will help to develop the children's awareness of a range of genres written for different purposes and audiences, for example there is a letter from Little Bo Peep, and Tommy Tucker's recipe book.

Shared reading and discussing the text

- Before reading the extract, discuss the title with the children. Who is Lucy Locket and why is this question for her? Sing and act out the traditional rhyme 'Lucy Locket lost her pocket...' with the children. Talk to them about things that people might keep in their pockets. You could show them the contents of your pocket (for example, a handkerchief) and ask the children to talk to a friend about the contents of their coat pockets. Start with the question *What's in your pocket (name of friend)?* Explain to the children that in this extract the characters are searching for a lost key.
- Read the extract and ask the children to identify characters and the stories/rhymes in which we usually find them, for example Captain Hook from the story *Peter Pan*. (It would be useful if you could provide copies of these related texts for children to look at in the class reading corner/library).
- Ask the children to predict the contents of each character's pocket. Make a list on the board of characters included in the extract (Lucy Locket, Pinocchio, Little Miss Muffet and Captain Hook). Remind the children that names begin with a capital letter.
- Talk about the structure and layout of the extract. Each verse is introduced with a question to the next character (*What's in your pocket, Pinocchio?*). Each verse is four lines in length and contains a word that rhymes with the character's name (*Pinocchio/bow*). Ask the children to spot these rhymes and identify the repeated pattern and the place where the rhyme occurs in each verse.

Activities

- Ask the children to suggest new characters from familiar stories and write new verses to include them in this story. Follow the structure identified when discussing the text. Create a pocket complete with contents that match the new character. For example, you could have a letter from the Big Bad Wolf apologising to the Three Little Pigs for destroying their properties, or an information book about spiders for Little Miss Muffet. Continuing this over several lessons will enable you to focus on different types of writing.
- Encourage the children to write letters to one of the characters; you can then respond in the guise of that character.

Extension/further reading

Make a Lucy Locket role-play area, complete with copies of the story and a rhyme, props and giant pockets for each character. Encourage the children to sort the props into the correct pockets and to label them. They could also write questions as clues to prompt each other when sorting props, for example *Who could a glass slipper belong to?*

Children will appreciate the similarities between *The Jolly Postman* by Janet and Allan Ahlberg (Heinemann Young Books) and this book. They may also like to read *Each, Peach, Pear, Plum* by Janet and Allan Ahlberg (Puffin) and *Once Upon a Time* by John Prater (Walker Books).

1: 1: T7: to re-enact stories in a variety of ways, e.g. through role-play, using dolls or puppets

1: 1: T10: to use rhymes and patterned stories as models for their own writing

1: 1: T14: to write captions for their own work, e.g. for display, in class books

What's in Your Pocket, Lucy Locket?

What's in your pocket,
Lucy Locket?

Just another pocket
Tied with a bow [R]
Let's go and ask
Pinocchio. [R]

What's in your pocket,
Pinocchio?

Only some plays
And a couple of puppets.
Let's go and ask
Little Miss Muffet.

What's in your pocket,
Little Miss Muffet?

Yuck! A dead spider
And a cookery book. [R]
Let's go and ask
Captain Hook. [R]

What's in your pocket,
Captain Hook?

Paul and Emma Rogers

repeated refrain is a question

gives opportunities for prediction

repeated in each 4-line verse

there is always a word that rhymes with the character's name

characters' names can be identified

question marks and exclamation marks help reader to interpret text

rhyming words

capital letters for names

1: 1: S4: to write captions and simple sentences, and to re-read, recognising whether or not they make sense, e.g. missing words, wrong word order

1: 1: W10: to recognise the critical features of words, e.g. length, common spelling patterns and words within words

Rules for the cloakroom

P 122

Background

This text provides a starting point for discussing typical features of instructional texts, such as the use of imperative verbs (sometimes referred to as 'bossy' verbs with young children) at the beginning of sentences, and the use of short, snappy sentences. Children can compare these rules with other forms of instructions, such as those found in recipes or for making models. Many schools display lists of rules indicating how children should behave or how they should look after property. The list of rules for the cloakroom can not only be used for shared reading but subsequently for shared writing as children devise their own rules. The text also offers opportunities for extensive work on CVC words.

Shared reading and discussing the text

- Read the rules together and discuss them. Ask the children if they agree with the rules and whether they would like to change any of them. Write any amendments on the board, using the children's ideas for phrasing.
- Discuss the way in which *please* is used and explain that it applies to all the rules. Help the children to see how this word makes the rules seem a little less unfriendly in tone. Talk about the use of imperative verbs at the beginning of each line, which is usually a key feature of rules and instructions.
- Write a set of rules for another area of the school, using the same style as for the rules for the cloakroom. Use the opportunity to talk about the use of imperative verbs and to show how a single word followed by a colon and a list can be applied to every item in the list. Try using alternatives to *please* such as *remember* or *don't forget to*.
- Look at CVC words with the children, highlighting them in the text: *peg, put, hat, bag, big, bin*. Sort these according to their initial sounds, then medial sounds, then final sounds. Generate rhyming strings such as *peg, beg, leg* and *hat, bat, fat, cat*.

Activities

- Provide pairs of children with CVC words on cards and ask them to sort the cards according to initial sounds (*beg, bat...*), medial sounds (*met, led...*) and final sounds (*rag, mug...*).
- Ask the children to play a matching game, finding the CVC words that rhyme (*cot, lot, pot...*) among a set of cards with CVC words on them.
- Give the children a cloze exercise based on a set of rules for a school activity. Ask them to use words from a word bank to complete the text by filling in the missing words. For example:

Stop ____ the whistle blows.
Line up quietly with your ____.
Wait for your ____.
Walk to ____ cloakroom.

when teacher class the

Extension/further reading

Link the activity to PSHE and citizenship for Key Stage 1 in which children are expected to agree and follow rules for their group and classroom and understand how rules help them. Discuss examples of rules which can be found in school and ask the children to tell you about rules for games they play at school or at home.

To write their own set of rules, the children could use a computer, possibly with the support of a writing program such as *Clicker*. This offers a selection of words for children to click on to enable them to complete sentences. Discuss the style in which rules should be presented, with imperative verbs at the beginning of each sentence. Help the children to decide what their rules are going to be about, for example a familiar game.

1: 1: T13: to read and follow simple instructions, e.g. for classroom routines, lists for groups in workbooks

1: 1: T16: to write and draw simple instructions and labels for everyday classroom use, e.g. in role-play area, for equipment

1: 1: W3: from YR to practise and secure the ability to hear initial and final phonemes in CVC words, e.g. _fit, mat, pan_

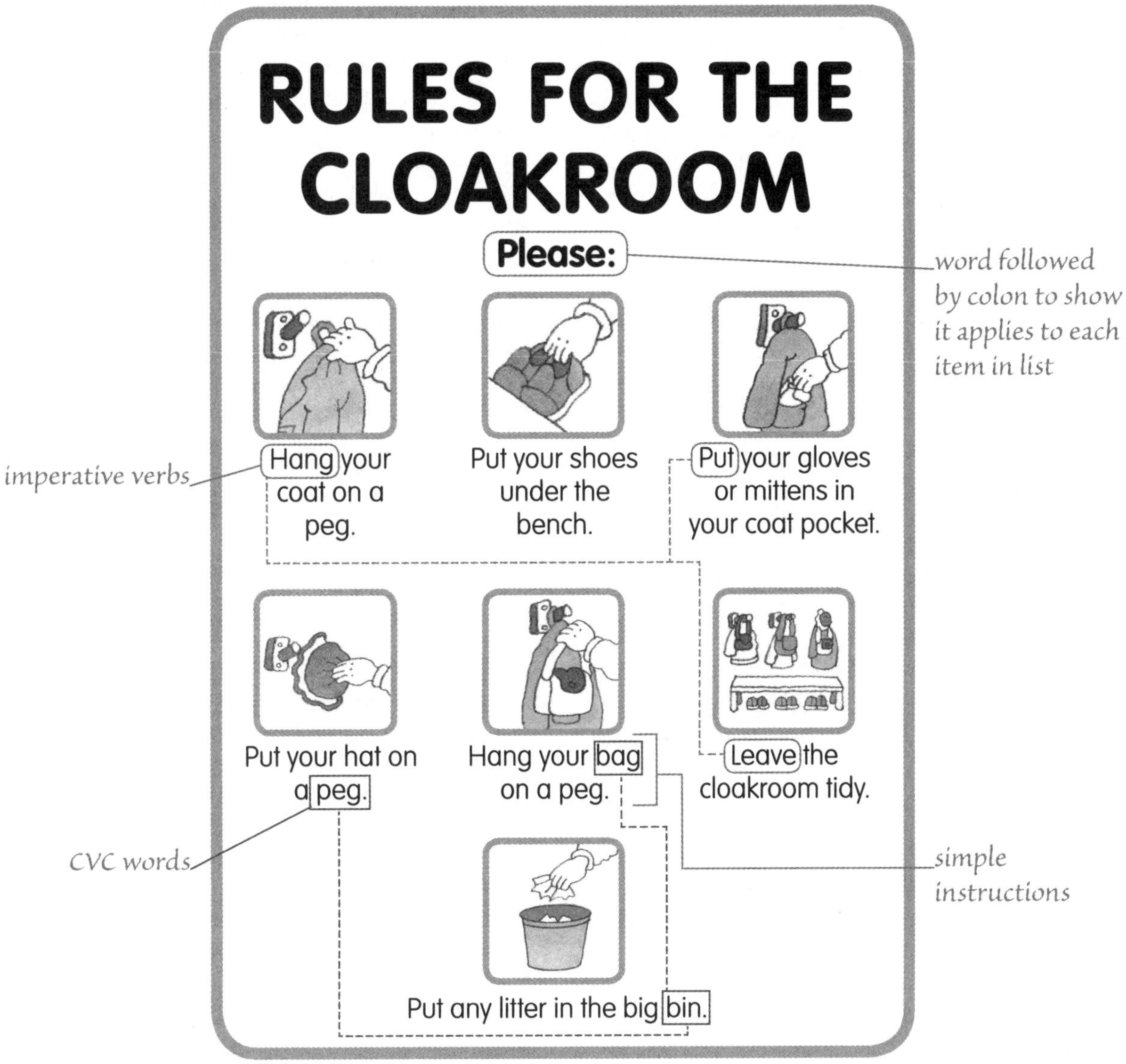

1: 1: W4: to discriminate and segment all three phonemes in CVC words

1: 1: W5: to blend phonemes to read CVC words in rhyming and non-rhyming sets

1: 1: W6: to represent in writing the three phonemes in CVC words, spelling them first in rhyming sets, then in non-rhyming sets

1: 1: W8: to read on sight other familiar words, e.g. children's names, equipment labels, classroom captions

Plan of a school

P 123

Background

This text can be used in shared reading as a means of developing children's word-level skills and ability to recognise familiar words. The activities will help to develop their familiarity with and understanding of environmental print. Links can be made with 'Rules for the cloakroom' (see page 34) and 'Labelled drawers' (see page 38), which also focus on texts in familiar environments.

Shared reading and discussing the text

- To introduce the idea of a plan to the children, arrange some items on a table top, then draw a representation of the table top on the board. Now draw representations of the items within your drawing of the table top and label them. Alternatively, draw and cut out representations of the items (put some Blu-Tack onto the back of each one), and ask the children to place them correctly on the plan of the table top.
- Look at the text with the children, explaining that it shows a plan of a school. Invite individuals to point to different parts of the school they can see. Discuss the way in which the plan is set out and labelled, with words being presented in different ways – that is, some are written vertically. Talk about words on the plan which may be unfamiliar to the children, for example *secretary, corridor* and *entrance*. Discuss how the words *headteacher* and *playground* can each be split into two separate parts to aid reading. If any of the words can be seen around the school, ask the children to look out for them next time they are moving from one room to another.
- Play an I-spy game with the children while they look at the plan. For example, *I'm thinking of a room which begins with st. What do you think it could be?* You may need to offer help by asking such things as *Could it be the cloakroom?* (emphasising the *cl* blend at the beginning of the word).
- Ask the children to study the plan and describe a route from one place to another. Encourage them to use sentences such as *Turn left as you leave Class 3* and *Walk along the corridor past Class 4*.

Activities

- Model labelling with the children by using labels for parts of the classroom and drawing an outline of the classroom on the board. Talk about the importance of presenting labels clearly so that they can be read easily and readers can see to which items they refer. It is important that they try to make their handwriting neat and accurate.
- Arrange some objects on a table top and ask the children to draw a plan and write labels for it, using a word bank for reference. They may also need help from an adult.
- Provide the children with an unlabelled plan of their school and a word bank. The word bank should comprise words for different parts of the school. Ask them to label the school plan. They can do this either by writing on the plan themselves or by using prepared labels.
- Ask the children to complete words that have some letters missing, for example *st_ffr_ _m, playgr_ _nd, cl_ssr_ _m*, using their developing phonological skills. The words can be written on small pieces of card or paper.
- Provide pairs of familiar words from the plan and others which children are likely to meet in the classroom and around the school and show the children how they can play a matching game. Ask them to turn all the words face down and then take turns to turn over a pair to try to make sets.

Extension/further reading

Ask the children to label other plans of familiar areas, for example a small section of their village or town, or their bedroom at home. If necessary, ask an adult helper to provide outlines to guide them.

1: 1: T12: to read and use captions, e.g. labels around the school, on equipment

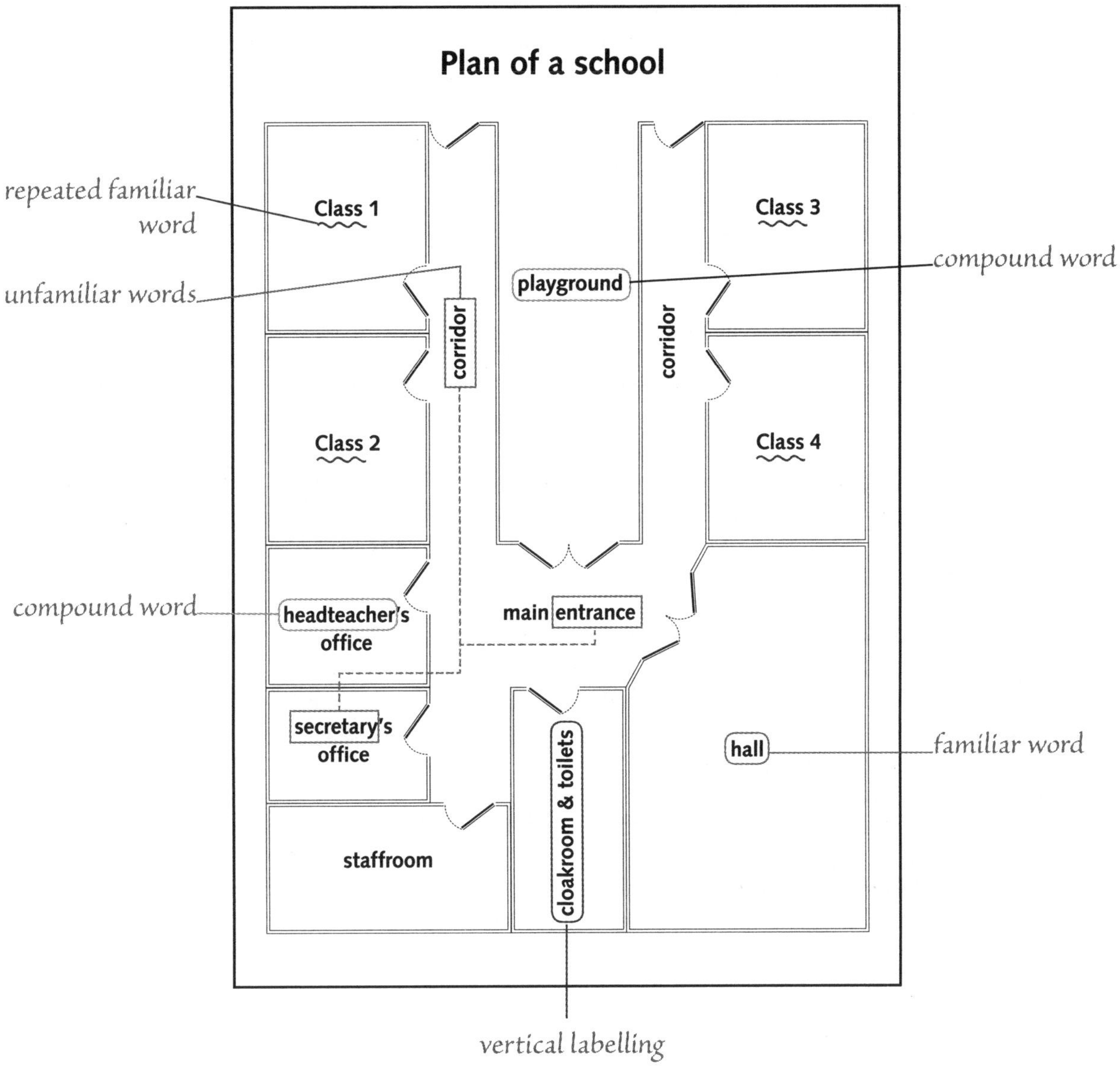

1: 1: W8: to read on sight other familiar words, e.g. children's names, equipment labels, classroom captions

1: 1: W12: to gather new words from reading and shared experiences, and to make collections of personal interest or significant words and words linked to particular topics

Labelled drawers

P 124

Background

Labels on drawers in the classroom will be familiar to most Key Stage 1 children. The drawers are usually plastic trays labelled with children's names or with useful items for the classroom. Most teachers have a few similar chests of drawers and spread children's trays among them in order to avoid congestion when everyone has to get things out at the same time; hence, the mixture of children's trays and equipment trays. This text can be used to develop children's word-recognition skills.

Shared reading and discussing the text

- Look at the text with the children and read the labels together. Talk about the reasons for labelling drawers and other items. Ask the children to find similar labels in the classroom.
- Can the children explain why some of the labels have capital letters while others are in lower case? Talk with them about the need to begin special names – in this case, names of people – with capital letters.
- Discuss the pronunciation of the words and the graphemes which represent them. Look at the regular phonemes first but go on to talk about the beginning of the word *scissors*. Talk about other words in which *sc* represents the *s* sound, such as *science, scientist* and *conscious*. Explain that this is unusual but that our language includes irregular sounds and that names are often spelled in irregular ways.
- Look at the spellings and relate these to sounds. Focus on the children's names, such as the *ay* sound in *Kate*. Discuss other names the children know and talk about how the same letters can represent different sounds, such as the *ch* in *Charlotte, Chloe* and *Charles*.
- Discuss with the children any unfamiliar phonemes, such as *ai* in *plain*.
- Talk about the different ways in which things can be labelled, comparing the text here with 'Plan of a school' (see page 36).

Activities

- Take some unlabelled trays and produce labels with the children's help, modelling careful writing of words.
- In guided reading, show the children examples of labels around the classroom and the school. Talk with them about the features and effects of clear labelling, such as the use of capital letters, large fonts and different coloured inks and backgrounds.
- Provide the children with a blank picture of a chest of drawers and a word bank of names and items to use to label them. Or ask them to copy from labelled drawers that they can see around them in the classroom.
- Discuss alphabetical order with the children and rearrange drawers in the classroom so that children's names are arranged, left to right, in alphabetical order, and equipment items are similarly organised.

Extension/further reading

Provide children with a simple picture to label, such as the different parts of a house or the parts of the body.

Distribute word cards to the children and ask them to find pairs of cards that have the same initial sounds on their cards. The cards could include the words *pencil, pen, paint, paper, chalk, chair, table, television, rubber, ruler, brush, book, apple, ant, house, home,* for example.

1: 1: W2: from YR, to practise and secure alphabetic letter knowledge and alphabetic order

1: 1: W8: to read on sight other familiar words, e.g. children's names, equipment labels, classroom captions

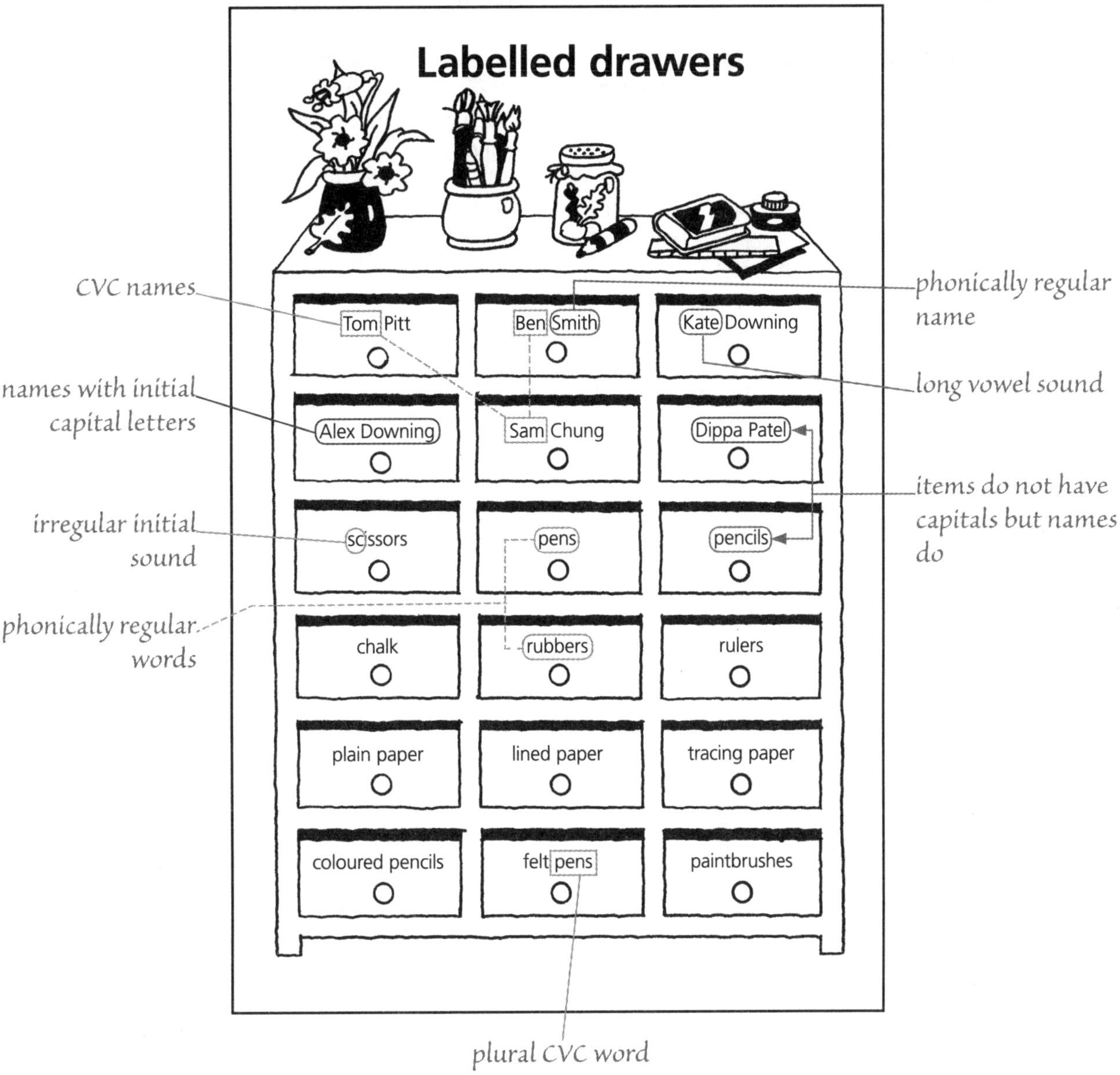

1: 1: W12: to gather new words from reading and shared experiences, and to make collections of personal interest or significant words and words linked to particular topics

1: 1: T12: to read and use captions, e.g. labels around the school, on equipment

1: 1: T16: to write and draw simple instructions and labels for everyday classroom use, e.g. in role-play area, for equipment

Animal lists

P 125

Background

Much of children's early writing takes the form of lists. Children may be used to seeing parents making shopping lists or lists to remind them of things to do. Similarly, they may have seen their teachers making lists, including those which remind children what they should be doing. The lists in this text provide opportunities to discuss classification and spelling. There are several animal names which are CVC words, so these may be used as starting points for work at word level.

Shared reading and discussing the text

- Read the lists with the children. Talk about any unfamiliar words and show how these may be sounded out. Try to avoid, where possible, adding an additional vowel sound when sounding consonants. It is less easy to achieve this with some letters and sounds, such as the *b* sound in *bag* and the *p* sound in *pig*, but children will find phonological decoding simpler if they are not confused into thinking that some consonants represent two sounds, leading them to write, for example, *bt* for *butter.*
- Look at the content of the lists. Discuss the role of headings and provide some other examples of headings which might be used to sort the animals, for example *Animals with four legs* or *Animals which can climb trees*. Ask the children in which lists they would place the other animals. Some may appear in more than one list, for example a mouse or rabbit could be either *Pets* or *Wild animals*.
- Look at words in the lists which may be unfamiliar to the children such as *guinea, stoat* and *squirrel.* Talk with the children about how they are spelled.
- Add more names of animals to the lists, modelling writing for the children and discussing the initial sounds of words and how these can be represented with letters.

Activities

- Ask the children to look at animals whose names are CVC words: *dog, cat, cow, pig, hen, fox, rat.* They should sort these according to their initial sounds, medial sounds and final sounds. They can then generate rhyming strings such as *hen, pen, ten* and *dog, log, fog.*
- Ask the children to make their own lists, using names of animals which have been written on cards or slips of paper. These could be placed under headings which are also on card or be pasted onto large pieces of paper adjacent to pictures of the animals. When the children have made their lists, show them how they can learn to spell the words by using strategies such as look, say, cover, write, check.
- Ask the children to arrange their lists in alphabetical order. To demonstrate this, use examples on the board or arrange cards with names of animals on them. Alternatively, give a group of children cards with their first names on them and ask them to come to the front of the class and to hold their cards in front of them. Ask the rest of the class to say which order the children need to stand in if they are to be in alphabetical order from left to right.

Extension/further reading

Ask the children to make lists of their own choosing. Suggest titles such as *Favourite songs* or *Favourite toys.* If they wish to make their own lists of animals, they could categorise them in different ways, for example dinosaurs could be grouped into *Carnivores, Omnivores* and *Herbivores*; or *Land-based, Water-based* and *Able to fly.* Some children could place their animal names in alphabetical order, with help from an adult. Ask the children to share their lists with partners or groups to explain how they decided to order or arrange the items in their lists.

1: 1: T15: to make simple lists for planning, reminding, etc.

1: 1: W1: from YR, to practise and secure the ability to rhyme, and to relate this to spelling patterns through:

- exploring and playing with rhyming patterns
- generating rhyming strings, e.g. *fat, hat, pat*

1: 1: W3: from YR to practise and secure the ability to hear initial and final phonemes in CVC words, e.g. *f̲it, m̲at, pa̲n̲*

Animal lists

Pets

dog

cat

guinea pig

hamster

Farm animals

cow

pig

horse

hen

Wild animals

deer

squirrel

stoat

hare

In which list does each of these animals belong?

Some may belong in more than one list.

rabbit

fox

sheep

mouse

rat

bull

CVC words (dog, cat)

unfamiliar word (guinea pig)

headings for lists (Pets, Farm animals, Wild animals)

CVC words (cow, pig, hen)

unfamiliar words (squirrel, stoat)

CVC words (fox, rat)

1: 1: W4: to discriminate and segment all three phonemes in CVC words

1: 1: W5: to blend phonemes to read CVC words in rhyming and non-rhyming sets

1: 1: W6: to represent in writing the three phonemes in CVC words, spelling them first in rhyming sets, then in non-rhyming sets

1: 1: W8: to read on sight other familiar words, e.g. children's names, equipment labels, classroom captions

Make a list

P 126

Background

It is important for children to see literacy with a recognisable purpose in an everyday setting, and this text comprises different types of lists. It can be linked to work on 'Labelled drawers' (see page 38) and 'Animal lists' (see page 40).

Shared reading and discussing the text

- Talk about lists and why people make them. Introduce the children to the different types of lists shown here – for reminders, for items to buy and for requests. Find other examples of lists (the class register, ingredients listed on packets, and so on) to share with the children.
- Read the 'Things to do' lists with the children and draw attention to the repeated words *Remember* and *Lock*. Invite the children to come to the front of the class and point to words which are repeated.
- Read the shopping list and the Father Christmas list. Examine the way all the lists are laid out, with only one phrase or word on a line. Ask the children why they think we only write a minimum of information in a list.
- Look at the language used in the lists, for example there are nouns in every item and sometimes they are accompanied by adjectives (for example, *magic*). In the 'Things to do' lists, imperative verbs are used (*Remember... Take... Pack...*). Talk about the difference between writing a list of tasks for ourselves and asking others to do tasks. For example, we would say *'Please would you put the cat out'* but would shorten it if we were writing down a quick reminder for ourselves. Point out that we use the word *please* when we wish to persuade others to do things, and that when we wish to remind ourselves to do something, or when we write instructions, we are not usually so polite!
- Use the lists to help children with recognition of high-frequency words. Highlight these.
- Look at common spelling patterns in some words, for example *pack* and *lock*. Ask the children to tell you how many phonemes there are in each word (three) and talk about which letters represent each sound.

Activities

- Make a list with the children's help showing some things you need to remember for the next day at school.
- Write a range of lists with the children, for example different lists of things to do such as weekly jobs in the classroom, and display these in the classroom.
- Ask the children to make their own lists, either in pairs or individually. Provide resources to support their activities, for example at the class shop you could have a supply of pre-made lists and a bank of words with corresponding pictures for the children to select items for their own lists.
- For more confident children, suggest they make more extensive lists from a wider range of topics. You could, for example, ask them to write a list of all the equipment in the technology trolley, or needed for a particular science topic.

Extension/further reading

Ask the children to make a collection of lists at home and to bring these into school to form part of a display. Display the lists with headings indicating the different types of lists (reminders, instructions and so on). Encourage the children to talk with parents and carers about the lists they use, and continue to add to the display as the children find more examples.

In guided reading, more confident readers will enjoy Pat Hutchins' *Don't Forget the Bacon!* and John Burningham's *The Shopping Basket* (both Red Fox).

1: 1: T15: to make simple lists for planning, reminding, etc.

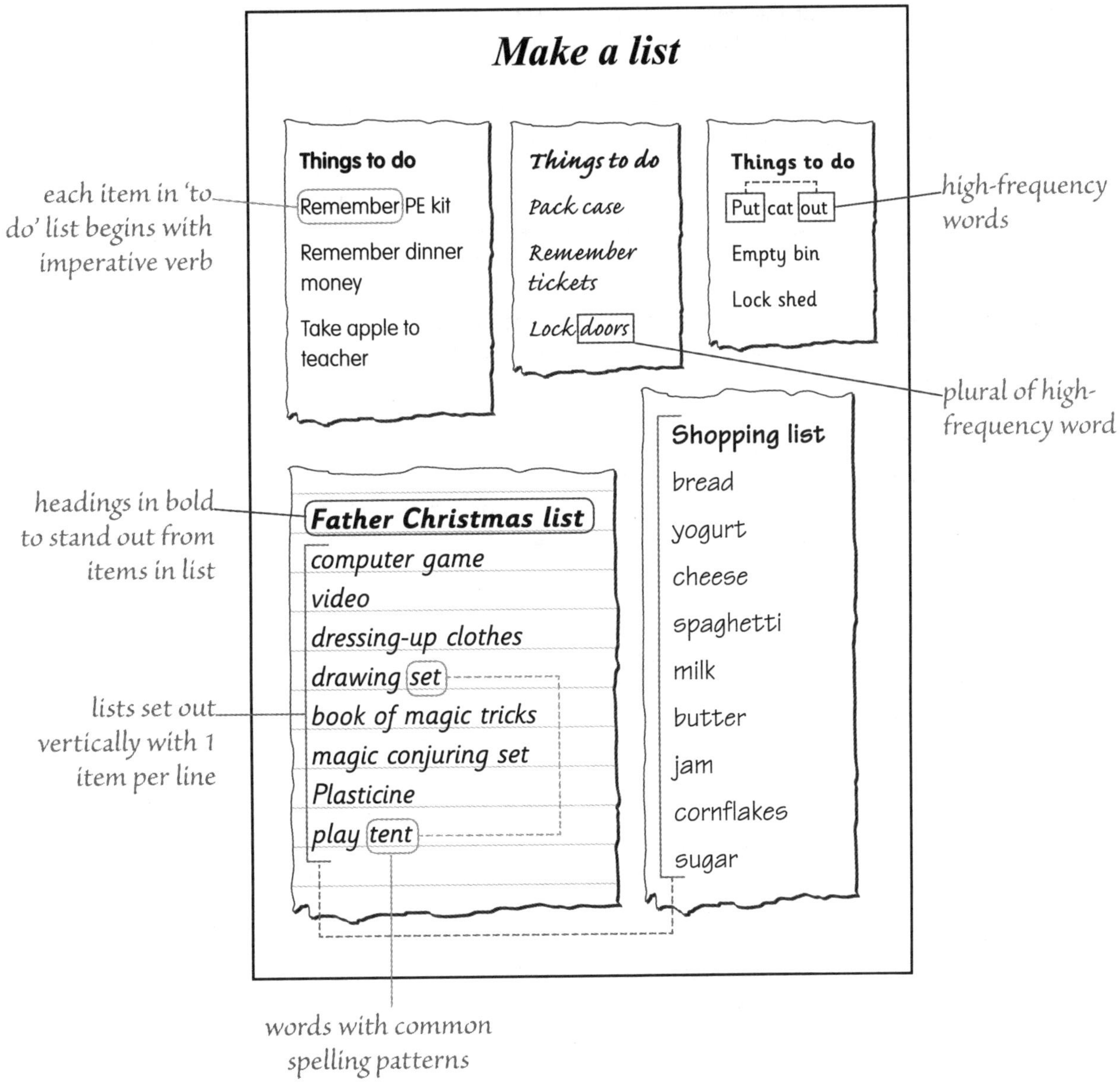

1: 1: W9: to read on sight approximately 30 high-frequency words identified for Y1 and Y2 from Appendix List 1

1: 1: W10: to recognise the critical features of words, e.g. length, common spelling patterns and words within words

Little Red Riding Hood retold by Tony Ross

P 127

Background

There are many versions of the story of Little Red Riding Hood, most of which have a rather more violent and less happy ending than this one. This extract is the fourth page of text from Tony Ross's book. The story features Red Riding Hood's father who, like a central character in 'The Three Wishes' (see page 48), is a woodcutter. This should enable you to compare themes and characters.

Shared reading and discussing the text

● Ask the children if they know the story of Little Red Riding Hood. Do they know how it begins? Discuss their ideas and, in shared writing, write the beginning of the story. Now read Tony Ross's version to the children. Compare it with the class story opening. Establish that the opening to the story provides the setting and introduces us to the characters. In Ross's version we are told that the father is a woodcutter, that the family live on the edge of the forest and that the grandmother lives deep in the forest. We are given clues about the characters, such as the father likes his daughter to help him cut wood so that he can *have a quiet smoke*, and the grandmother is *a nice, scatty old lady who was clever with her sewing machine* and made clothes including a red cape with a hood which the little girl wore whenever she went out on her bike.

● Make a list of key words that appear in the extract, such as *Grandma* and *Little Red Riding Hood.* Discuss the spellings of unfamiliar words, for example *afternoon, August, favourite, homemade, pickles, stout, programmes, straight* and *daydreams*, and have them clearly displayed during shared reading of the text. Ask the children to point them out in the text before you begin reading.

● After reading the text, look at some of the words again and talk about the clues which help us to know which words go where. Cover some of the unfamiliar words and read the text, inviting the children to suggest what the words should be and justifying their answers with reference to the semantics and grammar of sentences.

● Talk with the children about how this differs from more traditional versions. For example, the television guide that is referred to sets the story in a modern era.

Activities

● In guided writing, help the children to retell the story in their own words.

● Make a list of unfamiliar words for the children and ask them to learn some, using look, say, cover, write, check. Vary the number according to their abilities.

● Provide the children with the story in simple sentences with some words missing and ask them to use a word bank to help them to complete the sentences. For example:

Little Red Riding ______ lived in a forest.
Her mother packed some things in a ______.
She set off to visit her grandma's ______.

Extension/further reading

Many children will be familiar with different versions of 'Little Red Riding Hood'. Discuss the ones they know and encourage them to retell these orally, giving the main points in chronological order. If you have a copy available, go on to read the whole of Tony Ross's story to them and compare his ending with those they already know. If the book is not available, write an ending with the children in shared writing, trying to sustain the modern style which characterises Ross's version.

Roald Dahl's poetry version of the story in *Revolting Rhymes* (Puffin) is written in a modern style and is both engaging and amusing.

1: 2: T4: to retell stories, giving the main points in sequence and to notice differences between written and spoken forms in retelling, e.g. by comparing oral versions with the written text; to refer to relevant phrases and sentences

1: 2: S2: to use awareness of the grammar of a sentence to decipher new or unfamiliar words, e.g. predict text from the grammar, read on, leave a gap and re-read

title

Little Red Riding Hood

traditional story opening

One fine afternoon in August, the little girl's mum packed some of Grandma's favourite things in a bag: some homemade tarts and pickles, a bottle of stout, and the paper with the weekend television programmes in it. Little Red Riding Hood set off on her weekly visit to Grandma's house. Her parents walked down to the bottom of the field with her.

unfamiliar words

deviation from normal traditional story time setting

key words

"Hurry straight to Grandma's," they called, waving goodbye.

"Don't play about on the way, and don't lose yourself in daydreams!"

unfamiliar phrasing may require explanation

1: 2: S3: to predict words from preceding words in sentences and investigate the sorts of words that 'fit', suggesting appropriate alternatives, i.e. that make sense

1: 2: W10: to gather new words from reading and shared experiences and to make collections of personal interest or significant words and words linked to particular topics

The Frog Prince retold by Stephen Corrin

P 128

Background

This version of the Grimms' tale involves a princess losing her golden ball and having it retrieved by a frog to whom she makes a series of promises which, to her horror, then has to keep. Discussion of this story can be linked to work on other traditional tales in this term (see pages 44 and 48–54).

Shared reading and discussing the text

- Read the extract with the children and discuss events so far. Ask them if they know the story or have an idea about what might happen. Do they know of any other stories in which animals talk? Can they compare this story with other traditional tales?
- Discuss the characters with the children and ask them to describe the frog and the princess. Draw two columns on the board and ask the children to suggest adjectives which could be listed for each character. Talk with them about some of the adjectives used in the extract, then focus on *heartbroken* and *tear-stained.* Ask them what they think is meant by these terms and show them how each can be divided into two separate words.
- Look at some of the less familiar words, such as *splendid, sparkling, fountains, swiftly, croaking* and *gravely,* and show the children how they can use phonological, contextual, grammatical and graphic clues to predict and work out their meanings.
- Pick out some of the words which appear in high-frequency word list 1 and look at these with the children, ensuring that they can read them and, where appropriate, write them accurately, for example *one, once, there, had, many, very, little, girl* and *want.*

Activities

- Tell the rest of the story to the children – you could use the following outline.

The princess agrees to the frog's request and he retrieves her ball. The next day he turns up at the castle and, after the princess has explained the promise she made, her father, the king, tells her she must keep it. So she feeds the frog and then lets him sleep in her bed, although she sobs herself to sleep. When she wakes up, there is a handsome prince at the foot of the bed who explains that he was turned into a frog by a wicked witch and that only a beautiful princess can break the spell. The two become friends and when they grow up they marry and live happily ever after.

- In guided writing, help the children to make lists of characteristics of characters from the story to accompany pictures of the Frog and the Princess. Either provide the pictures for them or ask them to draw or paint their own in an art lesson.
- Ask the children to find examples in the text of a selection of high-frequency words and to highlight them.
- Ask more able children to write their own versions of the story, making use of words which were discussed earlier from high-frequency word list 1 and less familiar words which appear in the text.

Extension/further reading

Encourage the children to find examples of compound words such as *heartbroken* and *tear-stained* in other texts, dividing them into segments to read them.

Link the princess's reluctance to keep her promises to work in PSHE and citizenship.

Read other traditional stories to the children in *Sleeping Beauty and Other Classic Fairy Tales* by Charles Perrault (Gramercy Books). They may like to read the story of Cinderella in the Ladybird *Read it yourself* series.

1: 2: T6: to identify and discuss a range of story themes, and to collect and compare

1: 2: T8: to identify and discuss characters, e.g. appearance, behaviour, qualities; to speculate about how they might behave; to discuss how they are described in the text; and to compare characters from different stories or plays

The Frog Prince

Many years ago there lived a King and Queen who had an only daughter. She was very beautiful and loved playing with her friends in the royal park, which was full of splendid trees and sparkling fountains.

One day she took her friends out to play a game with her favourite golden ball. Once the lovely golden ball was just about to drop into the Princess's hands when suddenly the sun got in her eyes. The ball dropped to her feet and rolled swiftly into a well near by. The Princess ran forward and bent over the well, heartbroken to see her golden ball disappear into the dark green waters. She began to weep and when her friends tried to cheer her up she sent them away and just sat there alone, all sad and tear-stained.

Suddenly she heard a little croaking voice saying:

"What is the matter, little princess? Why is so beautiful a girl so sad?"

"Oh, froggie," she replied. "I am crying because my golden ball has fallen into the well."

"Never mind," said the frog, "I can easily dive down and fetch it up again."

"Can you really?" said the Princess. "Please do. I shall give you anything you wish to have if you bring me back my golden ball! Even my golden crown!"

"I do not want your crown," replied the frog gravely. "All I want is to sit by you and eat at your table, drink from your cup and sleep in your bed."

Annotations: title; typical opening for traditional story; language of time; unfamiliar words; indication of Princess's character; unfamiliar words; compound adjective; compound adjective; animal talking; unfamiliar word; CVC words

1: 2: S2: to use awareness of the grammar of a sentence to decipher new or unfamiliar words, e.g. predict text from the grammar, read on, leave a gap and re-read

1: 2: S3: to predict words from preceding words in sentences and investigate the sorts of words that 'fit', suggesting appropriate alternatives, i.e. that make sense

1: 2: W6: to read on sight approximately 30 more high-frequency words from Appendix List 1

The Three Wishes

retold by David Waugh

Extract 1

P 129

Background

This text, presented in two parts, is a traditional story with a clear series of events. It lends itself to discussion of characters and reasons for incidents. Some of the words will be unfamiliar to many children, and whole-class work on using phonological, contextual, grammatical and graphic clues to predict and work out their meanings would be helpful.

Shared reading and discussing the text

- Read the story opening with the children and talk about the way in which the woodcutter repeats himself. Talk about how this helps to convey his mood.
- Discuss the events so far. Ask the children what they would do if they were granted three wishes. Explain that you will be telling them the rest of the story later and that the wishes did not turn out as the woodcutter might have expected.
- Discuss the characters of the woodcutter and his wife. Why is the woodcutter unhappy? What does his wife say to try to help him? Why doesn't this work? Encourage the children to tell you what they think the characters are like. Explain that they will be finding out more about them in the second extract.
- Look at some of the unfamiliar words, such as *forest, branches, planks, furniture, wearily, grumbled, suddenly, pointed* and *pleaded*, and show the children how they can use phonological, contextual, grammatical and graphic clues to predict and work out their meanings. To demonstrate how to use contextual clues, for example, write a sentence on the board in which there is a completely wrong word which begins with the same letter as a more appropriate word, such as *The woodcutter cut down <u>toys</u> in the forest.* By doing this you will be able to show the children the importance of monitoring for meaning as well as looking at initial sounds when reading.
- Talk about the word *woodcutter*, which is a compound word and names the person in terms of an occupation.

Activities

- Talk about different story openings and look at examples in other stories. Ask the children to work in pairs and/or with adult helpers to write their own openings for the story of the three wishes. Share these in a plenary session and discuss the different possibilities.
- Provide the children with some adjectives which can be used to describe characters. Include some which would be appropriate for the woodcutter and for his wife and some which would not, for example *hard-working, happy, unhappy, tired, dirty, young, old* and *grumpy*. Ask the children to choose adjectives to describe each character and to write them on a piece of paper on which they have drawn a picture of the woodcutter on one half and his wife on the other.
- Provide a prediction exercise with simple sentences related to the story to complete:

The woodcutter worked hard all _____.
When he was cross, he often said things _____ times.
The woodcutter wished he did not have to work so _____.
The woodcutter's _____ told him to stop grumbling.
A tiny _____ asked the woodcutter not to cut trees down.

Extension/further reading

After telling the whole story to the children, ask them how the woodcutter came to have sausages on his nose and how he could have prevented this from happening. Ask the children to work in pairs to create an alternative ending to the story in which the wishes do not go wrong. How can they avoid the mistakes the woodcutter and his wife made? Alternatively, they could write about three wishes which cause equivalent chaos!

Compare 'The Three Wishes' with the extract from *Little Red Riding Hood* (see page 44), each story having a similar setting and a character who is a woodcutter.

1: 2: T7: to discuss reasons for, or causes of, incidents in stories

1: 2: T8: to identify and discuss characters, e.g. appearance, behaviour, qualities; to speculate about how they might behave; to discuss how they are described in the text; and to compare characters from different stories or plays

1: 2: T16: to use some of the elements of known stories to structure own writing

The Three Wishes

Extract 1

Long, long ago in a forest a voice could be heard.

"Trees, trees, trees," said the voice grumpily. "Chop, chop, chop, saw, saw, saw. All day long, every day, that's all I do."

The voice belonged to a woodcutter who lived with his wife in a little house next to a forest. The woodcutter worked hard all day cutting down trees. He sawed branches into logs for people to burn on their fires. He sawed the trunks of the trees into planks which could be used to make furniture. In fact, he cut down so many that there were spaces in the forest without any trees at all.

One evening, as he sat wearily in his chair after another hard day's work, the woodcutter said to his wife, "I'm sick of trees, trees, trees, chopping, chopping, chopping and sawing, sawing, sawing!"

His wife said, "Do stop grumbling, and I wish you wouldn't say everything three times when you're cross. It could be a lot worse. Some people don't have jobs or homes to live in."

But the woodcutter was not happy and every day he grumbled when he had to go to work and grumbled again when he got home. He grumbled while he was working, even though he was alone and no one could hear him. "Trees, trees, trees," he would mutter, "I'm sick of cutting them down and cutting them up."

K One day he was sitting on the stump of a tree which he had just chopped down, grumbling to himself about how hard his life was. Suddenly, he heard someone say, "Please don't cut any more trees down. The forest is disappearing and the birds and animals will soon have nowhere to live."

The woodcutter looked around and there, standing next to an oak tree, was a tiny man.

"I have to cut down the trees because if I don't my wife and I will not have enough money to buy food," he said to the little man, who was dressed all in green with a green pointed hat on his head.

The tiny man looked up at the woodcutter and pleaded, "Please don't cut any more trees down unless you plant some in their place. If you promise to do that, I will grant you three wishes."

"Three wishes?" said the woodcutter. "Now that sounds like a good thing. All right, I won't cut any more trees down."

"You have to make the wishes in your house or they won't work," the little man told him before he vanished.

The woodcutter could not wait to get home to make his wishes. He hurried through the woods and burst into the house, eager to tell his wife what had happened.

Annotations:

- *title* (The Three Wishes)
- *means that this is 1st part of story* (Extract 1)
- *typical traditional story opening* (Long, long ago in a forest)
- *repetition for effect* ("Trees, trees, trees," … "Chop, chop, chop, saw, saw, saw.")
- *unfamiliar word* (belonged)
- *unfamiliar word* (furniture)
- *language of time* (One evening)
- *indicators of character* (His wife said, …)
- *key event* (K)
- *language of time* (One day)
- *unfamiliar words* (Suddenly, is disappearing, pleaded, promise)
- *leaves reader wanting to find out more* (final paragraph)

1: 2: S2: to use awareness of the grammar of a sentence to decipher new or unfamiliar words, e.g. predict text from the grammar, read on, leave a gap and re-read

1: 2: S3: to predict words from preceding words in sentences and investigate the sorts of words that 'fit', suggesting appropriate alternatives, i.e. that make sense

1: 2: W10: to gather new words from reading and shared experiences and to make collections of personal interest or significant words and words linked to particular topics

The Three Wishes retold by David Waugh *Extract 2*

P 130

Background

This text is the concluding part of the story and should be done only after the children are familiar with extract 1 (see page 48).

Shared reading and discussing the text

- Remind the children of the events of the first part of 'The Three Wishes' and ask them to retell the story as a class.
- Read the first sentence of the continuation of the story: *'Where's the wood for the fire?' asked his wife as he walked in.* Look at the words *his* and *he* and ask the children to whom they think they refer. Read the next paragraph with them so that they can check if they were right. Talk about the way in which we can look beyond words we do not understand to look for clues about their meanings.
- Read the story to the children and talk about how it develops and how it ends. Ask them to identify the key events and make a list of these on the board. They could include: the woodcutter trying to dance with his wife; the woodcutter being hungry; the sausages on his lap; the sausages on his nose; the woodcutter and his wife trying to remove the sausages; the sausages vanishing; the woodcutter and his wife laughing.
- Discuss the characters of the woodcutter and his wife again after reading the end of the story and look back at the adjectives which were used to describe them in extract 1. Ask the children to add others in light of the events and discuss the reasons for any changes of mind about the characters.
- Look at some of the phonically regular unfamiliar words such as *supper, offering* and *disappeared.* Show the children how they can decode the words by breaking them into sections – *supp-er, off-er-ing* and so on.
- Look at the words ending with *ng,* such as *going, making, arguing, doing, planting* and *nothing.* Read the words with the children and ask them to tell you some other words ending in *ng.* Practise saying the words with them and talk about pronunciation.

Activities

- Ask the children to find examples of *ng* words in their reading books and to make a collection of them. Ask them to work together to practise pronouncing the words, and encourage them to break the words into segments to read them.
- Provide the children with a copy of the text in which you have covered up some of the words ending in *ng.* You could do this by using a dark marker pen on a photocopy to obliterate the words and then making further copies. Ask them to use the grammar of the text to determine which words are missing.
- When you have read the end of the story with the children, choose two good readers to read the dialogue for the woodcutter and his wife. Encourage them to be expressive, and talk with the class about how they think each line should be said.
- Ask the children to work in threes to produce short plays which re-enact the events of the second half of the story. One child should play the part of the woodcutter, one the woodcutter's wife, and one should narrate. Ask the children to perform their plays for the class. Discuss their interpretations and how these are similar to or different from the written version.

Extension/further reading

At the end of the story the woodcutter vows never to cut down another tree without planting one in its place. Talk with the children about the reasons for this and link it to work in PSHE and citizenship on things which improve and harm the environment.

Make a wall display of the story with a storyboard of the key events illustrated by the children. Write captions for the pictures, making sure that *ng* words appear frequently.

Other traditional stories include *The Old Woman Who Lived in a Vinegar Bottle* in the *All Aboard* series (Ginn) and 'The Fisherman and His Wife' in *Classic Tales* (OUP). *The Magic Finger* by Roald Dahl (Puffin) tells the story of a girl with magical powers.

1: 2: T4: to retell stories, giving the main points in sequence and to notice differences between written and spoken forms in retelling, e.g. by comparing oral versions with the written text; to refer to relevant phrases and sentences

1: 2: T9: to become aware of character and dialogue, e.g. by role-playing parts when reading aloud stories and plays with others

THE THREE WISHES

Extract 2

"Where's the wood for the fire?" asked the woodcutter's wife as he came in.

"I haven't brought any," replied the woodcutter, "but it's all right, I'll never need to cut wood again. You see, I met a little man in the woods and he told me that if I didn't cut any more trees down, he'd grant me three wishes. We're going to be rich!" And the woodcutter took his wife in his arms and tried to dance with her.

"Get off me, you stupid man!" she cried. "How can you be so daft? We need wood for the fire so that I can cook supper, but you haven't brought any. All you have managed to do is make up some silly story as an excuse for not doing your job. Well, I'm not making you any supper!"

The woodcutter decided it was not worth arguing with his wife so he sat in his chair and sulked instead. When supper time came he sat and watched as she ate bread and cheese without offering him any. He felt very hungry indeed.

"Oh I wish I had a string of tasty sausages!" he said, and suddenly he had. A string of sausages lay on his lap. His wife was furious.

"So you did have three wishes," she said. "Well what a stupid waste of a wish to ask for sausages. I wish they had landed on your nose!"

With that, the sausages flew through the air and stuck to the woodcutter's nose.

"So my wishes come true too," she said as her husband begged her to help get the sausages off his nose. They both pulled and pulled, but the sausages were stuck.

Finally, the woodcutter said, "Sausages, sausages, sausages! I wish they would disappear," and sure enough they did in a flash.

The woodcutter and his wife were sad that they had wasted their three wishes and had nothing to show for them, but as the days passed they began to see the funny side of what had happened. Whenever they thought about the sausages stuck on the end of the woodcutter's nose, they laughed until they cried. In fact, they were happier than they had ever been, and the woodcutter stopped saying things three times, worked hard at his job and took care never to cut down trees without planting others in their place.

Annotations:

- *part 2 of story* (Extract 2)
- *dialogue* ("Where's the wood for the fire?" asked the woodcutter's wife as he came in. / "I haven't brought any," replied the woodcutter,)
- *refers to woodcutter* (he)
- *indication of character* ("Get off me, you stupid man!" … any supper!")
- *unfamiliar words* (decided, arguing, sulked, furious, nothing)
- *phonically regular unfamiliar word* (offering)
- *phonically regular unfamiliar word* (disappear)
- *repetition (compare with extract 1)* (Sausages, sausages, sausages!)
- *'-ng' words* (nothing, saying, planting)
- *indication of changed character* (The woodcutter and his wife … in their place.)
- *environmental issue* (took care never to cut down trees without planting others in their place.)

1: 2: T14: to represent outlines of story plots using, e.g. captions, pictures, arrows to record main incidents in order, e.g. to make a class book, wall story, own version

1: 2: S2: to use awareness of the grammar of a sentence to decipher new or unfamiliar words, e.g. predict text from the grammar, read on, leave a gap and re-read

1: 2: W2: to investigate, read and spell words ending in *ng*

The Tortoise and the Hare

retold by David Waugh

P 131

Background

This story is one of Aesop's fables. Aesop was probably a slave on the island of Samos in Ancient Greece in the 6th century BC. His short stories, of which there are several hundred, often demonstrate the virtues of common sense and quick thinking. The characters are usually animals, the wolf, fox and lion featuring frequently. The story of the tortoise and the hare is a well-known story which should help children to develop their retelling skills, giving the main points in sequence.

Shared reading and discussing the text

- Read the story with the children and discuss the events. Some children may already know the story. If so, ask them to tell you about any differences between the versions they know and this text.
- Ask the children to describe the events in the story in sequence. As they do this, write sentences on the board such as *Hare said that Tortoise was slow. Hare asked Tortoise for a race. The race was started by Fox. At first Hare ran off ahead.*
- Talk with the children about the use of capital letters and full stops in sentences and explain that *Tortoise* and *Hare* have capitals because they are names.
- Look at words which may be unfamiliar to the children, such as *boasted, surprised, mumbled, plodded, steady, shady, towards* and *remembered,* and show them how they can use phonological, contextual, grammatical and graphic clues to predict and work out meanings.
- Focus on the sentences in the paragraph starting just below the initial dialogue (from *So Hare and Tortoise went to see Fox…*) and point out that they are demarcated by capital letters and full stops. Go on to look at the penultimate paragraph, but cover the punctuation marks for some sentences and ask the children to tell you which marks you have covered. Encourage them to look at the word which follows a punctuation mark to see if it begins with a capital letter so that they have a clue as to whether the mark is a full stop or a comma.
- Discuss the different characters of Tortoise and Hare. Ask the children how each of the animals might behave in different situations. For example, which one might rush his maths work and get lots of sums wrong, and which one might do his work more slowly but get it all right? Ask the children why they think the tortoise won the race when the hare was so obviously a faster runner.

Activities

- After telling the story to the children, ask them to fold a sheet of paper in half or draw a line down the middle of it. On one side, they should write *Tortoise*, and on the other *Hare*. Work with them to write sentences describing each of the characters, writing them in the correct column. For example, *Tortoise was slow. Hare could run fast. Hare was always boasting.*
- Give each child a piece of paper with six boxes on it in which they can draw pictures of the events in the story. Talk with them about the key events. Encourage them to write words and/or sentences to go with each picture.
- In shared writing, make use of the children's storyboards as a starting point for retelling the story. Begin by doing this orally, with the children making contributions. Occasionally, make deliberate errors and encourage them to pick up on them (for example, attribute the action of one character to another). Go on to write the story on the board, asking the children to help you to revise and edit it.

Extension/further reading

Children could go on to write or tell orally other stories with morals. This could be the theme for a class assembly or link to work in PSHE and citizenship.

The Very Best of Aesop's Fables by Margaret Clark and Charlotte Voake (Walker Books) is a collection in which the stories are told without the morals.

1: 2: T4: to retell stories, giving the main points in sequence and to notice differences between written and spoken forms in retelling, e.g. by comparing oral versions with the written text; to refer to relevant phrases and sentences

1: 2: T8: to identify and discuss characters, e.g. appearance, behaviour, qualities; to speculate about how they might behave; to discuss how they are described in the text; and to compare characters from different stories or plays

title

The Tortoise and the Hare

word written like this to emphasise meaning

unfamiliar words indicating character

key events

indicates character

capital letters to begin sentences

moral of story

"You are so slo-o-o-w!" said Hare as he watched Tortoise ambling along the road.

"I get to where I want to go soon enough," said Tortoise. "Sometimes you can get to places more quickly without rushing."

"Well you won't ever get anywhere quicker than me," boasted Hare.

"You might be surprised," said Tortoise slowly.

"So, do you think you can beat me in a race?" asked Hare.

"Maybe," mumbled Tortoise, "maybe."

K "Right, we'll have a race," said Hare, "and I'll beat you easily."

So Hare and Tortoise went to see Fox and asked him to make a start and a finishing line for the race. Then the two animals stood at the starting line waiting for Fox to say "Ready, Steady, Go!" As soon as he did, Hare dashed off towards the woods while Tortoise plodded along the path in his usual steady way.

After a few minutes, Hare thought that he would stop and have a rest. Tortoise will take hours to get to the finishing line, he thought. I'll sit under a shady tree and wait until he catches up and then I'll run to the finishing line and win the race.

K But Hare began to get drowsy as he lay in the shade of the tree and he soon fell asleep. After about an hour, Tortoise walked slowly past him without waking him and went along the path towards the finishing line. When Hare woke up he rubbed his eyes and remembered the race. He rushed along the path as fast as his legs would carry him, but, by the time he reached the K finishing line, Tortoise had already won the race and was sitting under a shady tree waiting for him.

"I told you," he said, "I get to where I want to go soon enough. Sometimes you can get to places more quickly without rushing."

1: 2: S2: to use awareness of the grammar of a sentence to decipher new or unfamiliar words, e.g. predict text from the grammar, read on, leave a gap and re-read

1: 2: S6: to use the term 'sentence' appropriately to identify sentences in text, i.e. those demarcated by capital letters and full stops

The Three Little Pigs by Marian Swinger

P 132

Background

This is a poetic retelling of the traditional story and has a rather less gory ending than many other versions. It follows the same pattern as the traditional story and makes use of repetitive language. Children often enjoy joining in with the text, and there are many opportunities to discuss language, wordplay and actions.

Shared reading and discussing the text

- Begin by discussing the story of the three little pigs and asking the children to tell you the versions they know. Write an outline of the story on the board based upon the information they provide. Add small sketches, captions and arrows for clarification of the storyline.
- Explain that the poem is written in pairs of lines that rhyme. Ask the children to follow the poem as you read it to them, but invite them to complete some of the rhyming couplets by pausing slightly just before the final word of the second line each time. For each couplet, encourage the children to predict the word by using the word at the end of the first line of the couplet.
- Discuss the spellings of the rhyming pairs of words. Encourage the children to notice that sometimes the cluster of letters which rhymes with another word may be spelled differently and sometimes the same. For example, *straw* and *door; more* and *straw; red* and *said; puff* and *enough* have rimes which sound the same but are spelled differently, while *in* and *grin; nap* and *tap; tricks* and *bricks, Now* and *Ow; smoke* and *poke* have rimes which are spelled the same.
- Compare the version of the story which is recounted in the poem with the composite version produced by the class that you wrote on the board. Where there are differences, ask the children to say which version they prefer and why. Discuss the ending, contrasting it with the wolf hobbling home in Swinger's version.

Activities

- Learn the poem as a class, with children being responsible for different lines, and recite it with actions, perhaps for a class assembly.
- Provide the children with sets of word cards which can be sorted into pairs of rhyming words. Include words that appear in the poem, but add other similar ones to reinforce familiarity with sound–symbol correspondence, for example, *straw, raw, draw, floor, thin, lap, brow, how, joke* and *huff.* Ask groups of children to sort the cards into pairs. Encourage them to experiment with other possible rhymes for the words, to add to their rhyming pairs. Ask an adult helper to work with them to write down their words on blank cards.
- In guided writing, help the children to retell the story, beginning by using a story map which represents graphically the journey of the three little pigs from house to house.
- Ask more able children to make lists of rhyming words, starting off each list with words from the poem. Encourage them to note whether the rhyming parts of the words are spelled the same.

Extension/further reading

Revolting Rhymes by Roald Dahl (Puffin) includes Dahl's version of the story of the three little pigs in poetic form. Read it to the children and discuss the differences between Dahl's and Swinger's versions. *The True Story of the Three Little Pigs* by Jon Scieszka (Puffin) is told by the wolf. After reading Scieszka's version to the children, discuss how the wolf's telling of the story differs from the text here.

Link these activities to science, 'Materials and their properties', in which children learn to recognise materials and find out about their properties and uses. Have a collection of straw, sticks and bricks in the classroom to enable the children to examine their properties and suitability as building materials.

1: 2: T4: to retell stories, giving the main points in sequence and to notice differences between written and spoken forms in retelling, e.g. by comparing oral versions with the written text; to refer to relevant phrases and sentences

1: 2: T11: to learn and recite simple poems and rhymes, with actions, and to re-read them from the text

title

The Three Little Pigs

3 key events

K1 The first little pig in a house of straw R
heard a tap tap tap on her little green door. R
"Little pig, little pig, let me come in,"
said the big bad wolf with a big bad grin.
Then he huffed and he puffed and he huffed some more
and down went the little pig's house of straw.
K2 The next little pig was taking a nap R
in her house of sticks when she heard a tap R
and the big bad wolf with a big bad grin R
gave a huff and a puff and blew her house in. R
K3 Then the big bad wolf, still up to his tricks, R
went off to the third little house of bricks. R
"Little pig, little pig, let me come in,"
said the big bad wolf with a big bad grin.
And he huffed and he puffed till his face turned red.
"My house is too tough," the little pig said. R
"I'll come down the chimney," the wolf yelled, "Now!"
But the fire was lit and the wolf yelled, "Ow!" R
and shot straight out in a cloud of smoke
as the third little pig gave the fire a poke. R
The wolf blew on his paws with a huff and a puff
and he hobbled off home. He'd had enough.

Marian Swinger

rhyming words that have rimes with different spellings

familiar phrases – these appear in most versions of the story

repeated phrasing

rhyming words that have rimes with matching spellings

final word in each pair of lines that rhyme – reader can predict what these are

story ending varies in different versions

author

1: 2: T14: to represent outlines of story plots using, e.g. captions, pictures, arrows to record main incidents in order, e.g. to make a class book, wall story, own version

1: 2: W3:
- to blend phonemes in words with clusters for reading
- to segment clusters into phonemes for spelling

1: 2: S3: to predict words from preceding words in sentences and investigate the sorts of words that 'fit', suggesting appropriate alternatives, i.e. that make sense

Half a Moon and One Whole Star

by Crescent Dragonwagon

P 133

Background

This extract, from a longer poem spread over several illustrated pages, focuses on a child called Susan and what happens during the night while she sleeps. The text here comprises the final page of the book and is written in rhyming couplets. Some of the language in the poem is quite complex and there are examples of unfamiliar phrasing which may need to be explained to the children.

Shared reading and discussing the text

- Read the extract to the children. Look with them at the name of its author. Ask if they think that Crescent Dragonwagon is a real name.
- Discuss the central image of night-time in the poem – the half moon and the whole star – and what the children understand by them. Talk about the description of the sun and the way in which the author uses a simile to liken it to a ball.
- Note the use of repetition (*Hang...; Sleep, Susan, sleep*) and rephrasing of the same ideas. Help the children to see how this enhances the poetic effect.
- Write with the children a description of the sun in rhyming couplets. Discuss the spellings of words they suggest.
- Look at other words with simple spellings which do not appear in the high-frequency lists. Discuss their spellings and whether they rhyme, for example *far/star; moon/soon.*
- Encourage the children to talk about what they think happens at night when they are asleep or to describe an experience of being awake at a time when they would usually be asleep. Some may have travelled through the night on family holidays or may be able to remember occasions when they have been woken unexpectedly. What sort of images of the night did they have? Write some of the children's suggestions and key vocabulary on the board.

Activities

- Focus on high-frequency words in the text, such as *ball, night, there, half* and *have*. Talk about their spellings and encourage the children to use look, say, cover, write, check to learn how to write them. Provide the children with whiteboards on which to write the words, so that you can check whether they have spelled them accurately.
- Ask the children to make lists of words and phrases which make them think about night-time. Use these as a staring point for shared writing about night, modelling correct spelling and emphasising the importance of using phonic knowledge to help to make intelligent guesses about spelling. For example, show the children how you can try out alternative spellings when you are uncertain and see which one looks right, then check in a simple dictionary to see if your guess was correct.
- Provide the children with a writing frame and ask them to fill in alternate lines in the poem, each line beginning with a capital letter. Less able children could fill in missing words. In both cases, children should work with partners to ensure discussion and sharing of ideas.
- More able children could write their own sentences about night-time using, as a starting point, some of the words and phrases suggested when discussing the text.

Extension/further reading

Read the whole poem, if it is available, and discuss the images of night-time. Provide other texts which feature descriptions of night-time or have night-time as a theme and encourage the children to look for ideas to help them with their own writing. Examples are the nursery rhyme 'Twinkle Twinkle Little Star', *This is the Bear and the Scary Night* by Sarah Hayes (Walker Books), The *Owl Who Was Afraid of the Dark* by Jill Tomlinson (Mammoth) and *Owl Babies* by Martin Waddell (Walker Books).

1: 2: T12: through shared and guided writing to apply phonological, graphic knowledge and sight vocabulary to spell words accurately

Half a Moon and One Whole Star

Up above the earth so far
Hang half a moon and one whole star
Hang one whole star and half a moon:
Night-time will be coming soon.
But where there's night there's day to follow
Sleep Susan sleep, for come tomorrow
Above the earth there will be one
Hotly glowing summer sun
Round and orange, like a ball
Like moon and star, you'll have them all!
So sleep, Susan, sleep.

Crescent Dragonwagon

each line begins with a capital letter

depicts images of moon and star at night

high-frequency words from list 1

repetition for poetic effect

describes sun

author's name – is it real?

rhymes with simple phonically regular spellings

simile

1: 2: T13: to substitute and extend patterns from reading through language play, e.g. by using same lines and introducing new words, extending rhyming or alliterative patterns, adding further rhyming words, lines

1: 2: W6: to read on sight approximately 30 more high-frequency words from Appendix List 1

1: 2: W9: to spell common irregular words from Appendix List 1

Weather

by Eve Merriam

P 134

Background

'Weather' is a contemporary poem that relies on the use of onomatopoeia to evoke the sound of the rain. The characteristics of raindrops are explored as the poet describes the action of the rain hitting the windowpane, making the reader feel glad to be safe and dry indoors. The pace and rhythm become faster as the number of syllables in each verse increases until the crescendo in the last verse when the tongue-twisting phrases are brought to a halt with a jump in a puddle.

Shared reading and discussing the text

- Read the poem to the children and tell them that it was quite tricky to read. Ask them to repeat each line in the first verse after you. Why is it difficult to read? If it happens to be a rainy day you could pause at this point to listen to the rain hitting the classroom windows. Discuss the irregular, jerky, snappy sound and relate this to the words and phrases in the text, for example *Dot a dot dot dot, Spack a spack speck.*
- Talk about the words that rhyme in the poem. Sometimes these words are at the end of a line, such as *windowpane/rain*; sometimes we can hear a rhyme within the same line, for example *spatter, scatter, clatter.* Discuss how this rhyme and rhythm helps the reader to imagine the rain hitting the window.
- Ask the children to clap along with the rhythm of the poem. Can they hear different numbers of syllables in different words? Once this has been established, children can be given percussion instruments which can be played loudly or softly to represent different types of raindrop throughout the poem.
- Ask the children to find words ending in *ck* and to think of more that rhyme. List words in a column to highlight the onset and rime, for example *b-ack; st-ack.*
- Talk about the patterned language in the poem. Read the first line of each verse with the children so that they can hear the similarities. Explain that the poet has used alliteration to speed up the pace of each line and has chosen some nonsense words which fit with the sound of the line rather than words that make sense, for example *A spatter a scatter; Slosh a galosh; Bumbershoot barrel; flick a flack fleck Freckling...* Talk about the meaning of these words in the context of the poem.

Activities

- Take the rhyming pairs that can be found in the poem, such as *windowpane/rain, glide/slide*, and write them on cards (one word on each card). Give out these words to the children and ask them to find their rhyming partner by calling out the word. Once found, pairs of children can make a list of more words that share the same rhyme. Draw the children's attention to words that sound the same but are spelled differently, for example *-pane/rain.*
- Extend the children's vocabulary by using the poem as a springboard to brainstorm ideas. Start by exploring the word *raindrops.* What do raindrops do? *Raindrops... spatter, splash, fall, glisten.* Extend this gradually to include an adjective, noun and verb, for example *Heavy raindrops splatter.* Then ask the children to describe *how* (this will encourage them to think of an adverb), for example *Soft raindrops fall gently.* Create a word bank in this way, then ask the children to rearrange the words in a different order to form new sentences.
- Encourage the children to help you write another line to extend the first verse, using the pattern, rhyme and rhythm that has been established.
- Ask the children to work in pairs to make a list of words in the poem beginning with the following consonant clusters: *sp, sl and fl.* How do we blend these letters together when reading? Can the children add more words to each list? Ask them to make a list of words containing the digraphs *sh* and *th.*

Extension/further reading

Read the poem 'Little Raindrops' by Jane Euphemia Browne in *Time for a Rhyme* chosen by Fiona Waters (Orion Children's Books).

1: 2: W1: to secure identification, spelling and reading of initial, final and medial letter sounds in simple words

1: 2: W2: to investigate, read and spell words ending in *ck*

1: 2: W3: to discriminate, read and spell words with initial consonant clusters, e.g. *bl, cr, tr, str* – Appendix List 3

1: 2 W7: to recognise the critical features of words, e.g. length, common spelling patterns and words within words;

WEATHER

Dot a dot dot dot a dot dot
Spotting the windowpane.
Spack a spack speck flick a flack fleck
Freckling the windowpane. R

A spatter a scatter a wet cat a clatter
A splatter a rumble outside.
Umbrella umbrella umbrella umbrella
Bumbershoot barrel of rain. R

Slosh a galosh slosh a galosh
Slither and slather a glide 2
A puddle a jump a puddle a jump
S A puddle a pump aluddle a dump a
Puddmuddle jump in and slide! 5

Eve Merriam

repetition speeds up pace and rhythm of poem and mimics the jerky, spasmodic sound of the raindrops

'ck' words

wordplay – words that don't make sense but are used for the way they sound

onomatopoeia

alliteration

consonant clusters/ blends

number of syllables in line increases

short vowel sound (medial sound) in CVC word

onset

rime

rhyming words with different spellings

in verse 3 there are rhymes within same line and at end of 2nd and 5th lines

1: 2: S3: to predict words from preceding words in sentences and investigate the sorts of words that 'fit', suggesting appropriate alternatives, i.e. that make sense

1: 2: T1: to reinforce and apply their word-level skills through shared and guided reading

1: 2: T11: to learn and recite simple poems and rhymes, with actions, and to re-read them from the text

1: 2: T13: to substitute and extend patterns from reading through language play, e.g. by using same lines and introducing new words, extending rhyming or alliterative patterns, adding further rhyming words, lines

Whose is it?

by Charles Thomson

P 135

Background

This extract provides a very basic playscript. It can be used to develop the children's understanding of the script format and to provide opportunities for role-play, both through using the text and through improvisation. The interaction between the characters may be very familiar to Year 1 children and could lead to discussions about arguing, the children being made aware of the 'twist' at the end of the dialogue.

Shared reading and discussing the text

- Discuss how the text is set out. Talk about the title, cast list and production notes and discuss the purpose of each. Ask if anyone can tell the class which words are spoken by A at the beginning of the dialogue. Talk about scripts and explain that these are used to guide actors when they perform plays and television dramas.
- Read the playscript to the children, with a good reader taking one part and you the other. If possible, practise this with the child before the lesson begins to ensure fluency and expression.
- Discuss with the children why they think A and B suddenly change their minds in the last two lines of the script about who owns the item. What do the children think the item, which is unspecified, might be? Can they suggest what A and B might be arguing about?
- Ask the children to provide you with further lines for the script and write these on the board, modifying them in light of their suggestions.

Activities

- Look at the common irregular words in the playscript: *one, yours, know, wrong, two, you.* Help the children to read these and to use look, say, cover, write, check to help them to learn how to write them. Provide the children with whiteboards on which to write the words so that you can check their spellings.
- Look at high-frequency words within the text and ensure that the children can read and spell them, for example *is, my, this, one, here*. Ask them to track for examples of these words in the text, providing them with a copy of the page and a highlighter pen so that they can identify and mark the words, enabling you to monitor their ability to find and read the words.
- In guided writing, help the children to write their own simple scripts. They could base these on dialogues between characters in stories which they have recently read. Traditional stories in which dialogue is presented, such as 'The Tortoise and the Hare' (see page 52), will give them the opportunity to turn direct speech into a playscript format.
- More able children could work in pairs to write their own scripts and prepare to perform them for the rest of the class. Encourage them to adopt roles and learn their lines.

Extension/further reading

Provide further examples of playscripts for the children and discuss the storylines as well as the layout and the role of stage directions.

Link the text here to discussions in PSHE and citizenship on resolving arguments – finding alternative ways of settling disputes, such as learning to share. Remind the children about 'The Three Wishes' (see pages 48 and 50) in which an argumentative couple waste an opportunity.

For further discussion of the three wishes theme, read 'The Third Wish' in *A Handful of Gold* by Joan Aiken (Red Fox).

1: 2: T7: to discuss reasons for, or causes of, incidents in stories

1: 2: T9: to become aware of character and dialogue, e.g. by role-playing parts when reading aloud stories or plays with others

title

Whose is it?

cast list

Characters
Two children.

production notes to give background information

Production notes
The two speakers in this dialogue are arguing over an unspecified object.

denotes who is speaking

exclamation marks help reader/actor to use appropriate expression

A: This is my one!
B: No, it's not!
A: It is! It's the one I got!
B: No, it isn't – look here! See...
A: It's the one that was given to me.
B: It isn't yours: I can show...
A: It's mine! It is! I know!
B: Don't pull – it's not very strong!
A: I want it. I'm right – you're wrong.
B: It's yours. Look: it's broken in two.
A: It's not mine: it belongs to you.

'twist' – characters change their minds as soon as object is broken; it is not wanted any more

common words with irregular spellings

1: 2: W6: to read on sight approximately 30 more high-frequency words from Appendix List 1

1: 2: W9: to spell common irregular words from Appendix List 1

From seed to sunflower by Dr Gerald Legg

P 136

Background

This extract is from a series of books called *Lifecycles* which aims to provide accurate information in a simple way about the processes of growth and change. The extract contains many of the features associated with non-fiction and provides a useful vehicle for introducing children to structural guides found in information books. It will also help them to become familiar with some of the language features typical of a report, for example an opening general statement, facts about the subject, a description using precise technical language, and a formal style usually written in the present tense.

Shared reading and discussing the text

- Before reading the text, ask the children if they know what a sunflower is. Can they describe one? Has anyone in the class ever grown a sunflower before? How do sunflowers start life?
- Explain that you are going to read a text that will give them information about this topic. Look at the title of the text and read it together. Explain that this piece of writing is a factual report, not a story, about how sunflowers grow from tiny seeds.
- Read the first sentence to the children. Discuss what time of year autumn is. What happens to the leaves on some trees during autumn?
- Read the next sentence, then give the children some sunflower seeds to look at and hold. Ask them what the text tells us is inside these seeds (two things: the tiny plant and the food the plant will need). Encourage the children to locate this information by re-reading the text.
- Read the next part of the extract to the class and talk about how the seeds become buried in the soil. (If appropriate, talk about the different ways seeds can be dispersed, for example by animals, by the wind, by falling to the ground and becoming buried in the soil.)
- Discuss the scientific words (technical vocabulary) introduced in the text – *minerals* and *germination*. Ask the children how we can find out what they mean. Write the definitions on the board. (Children may suggest looking in a dictionary and even though that is a good idea you can take the opportunity to introduce the glossary.)
- Ask the children to talk to a partner for one minute. They should tell each other a fact they have just found out about sunflower seeds. Ask the class what they would like to find out about sunflowers next. Discuss how they could research this topic.

Activities

- Ask the children to represent the information they have gained from reading the extract in a labelled diagram. Prompt them to answer the following questions:
  - Where do the seeds come from?
  - What is inside each seed?
  - Where do the seeds become buried?
  - What helps the seeds to grow?
- Once completed, ask the children to share their pictorial representations in small groups. Encourage them to discuss what they have learned about sunflower seeds.
- During guided group work, read the planting instructions on the back of a sunflower seed packet. Talk about why the seed needs to be buried beneath the surface of the soil. Ask the children to work in pairs to write their own glossary definitions for the words *seed* and *soil.* (If possible, children could go on to plant their own sunflower seed during a science lesson in order to put theory into practice and to apply their knowledge.)

Extension/further reading

Examine a different type of seed (for example, a seed with a different dispersal method – one with hooks, or one that floats to the ground) and write a class report in the style of 'From seeds to sunflower'.

Further reading includes *Eating Plants* by Rhonda Jenkins in the *All Aboard* series (Ginn).

1: 2: T17: to use terms 'fiction' and 'non-fiction', noting some of their differing features, e.g. layout, titles, contents page, use of pictures, labelled diagrams

From seed to sunflower

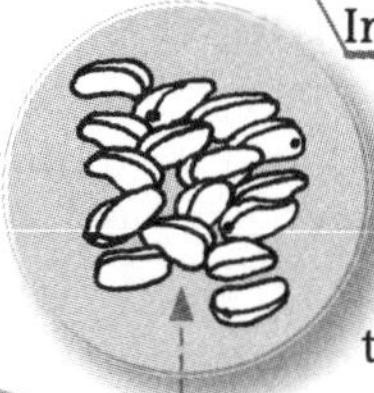

In autumn the seeds of fully grown sunflowers fall to the ground. A seed contains the tiny plant and the food the plant will need before it starts to grow.

The seeds are buried in the soil. The soil contains minerals. Minerals are special foods that help the plant to grow. In spring the warm sun and rain make the seeds begin to grow. This is called germination.

Sunflower words

Germination
The stage in the life cycle of a plant when the seeds first begin to grow.

Minerals
Special food in the soil. Plants need minerals to help them grow.

Annotations:

- *general opening statement*
- *diagram*
- *present tense*
- *formal style*
- *precise technical language*
- *linking verbs*
- *subject-specific terminology*
- *glossary defines unfamiliar words*
- *factual style; defines 'seed'*
- *diagram*

1: 2: T18: to read non-fiction books and understand that the reader doesn't need to go from start to finish but selects according to what is needed

1: 2: T22: to write labels for drawings and diagrams, e.g. growing beans, parts of the body

Keeping fit

by Paul Bennett

P 137

Background

This is an information text which conveys a lot of information clearly and concisely with the help of a labelled illustration. This makes the information more appealing than if it were a page of unillustrated text.

Shared reading and discussing the text

- Read the text with the children and discuss what is written about the value of exercise. Ask them if they know where their heart and lungs are and what functions these organs have.
- Look at the way in which the text is set out and talk about labelling. Draw the children's attention to the lines that have been drawn from the parts of the body to their names and explain that this makes the diagram tidier and clearer because the labels do not have to be written over the picture. Talk about the use of a different-sized font for the title and bold type for key words in the main part of the text.
- Look at the two sections which are presented in sentence form. Talk about their function in providing explanation. Ask the children if the labelled diagram on its own would warrant the title 'Keeping fit'.
- Ask the children to take turns to come out to the front of the class to use a pointer to indicate different parts of the body on the picture.
- Talk about the spellings of the parts of the body. Most are phonically regular but you will need to discuss the spellings of *knee* and *thigh* which may confuse some children. Focus on final consonant clusters in *hand, chest* and *neck*, and talk about other words which have the same clusters.
- Discuss the use of the present tense in the text. Most stories are written in the past tense and children may be more used to this format.

Activities

- Ask the children to draw their own pictures of people and to label them. Provide a bank of relevant words, including all those used here. Encourage more able children to label their picture in more detail, including the person's face, using labels such as *hair, eyes, nose, mouth, chin, ears* and *cheeks*. Provide them with reference texts in which they can find the words in order to spell them accurately.
- To reinforce children's ability to recognise and spell the words, make cards of pairs of words and ask them to match these.
- Take some cards on which you have written different parts of the body and give one set to each group of children. Ask them to place the cards face down on their table. They should then take it in turns to turn over a word card and ask others in their group to read it. If a child is able to read the word correctly, he or she can take the card and score a point.
- Talk with the children about keeping fit and discuss what is written about the value of exercise. Ask them to draw pictures of people taking different forms of exercise and to write simple sentences to accompany them.
- In guided writing, help the children to write simple sentences about their bodies. For example: *I have eight fingers and two thumbs. I have two elbows.*
- Ask the children to make up questions to go with the photograph of the boy, such as *How many knees does the boy have? Can you point to his ankle?*

Extension/further reading

Link the activities to work in PSHE and citizenship, or 'Life processes and living things' in science in which children are expected to group living things according to observable similarities and differences.

Display a collection of labelled pictures and diagrams. Provide activities which involve matching words from cards to those on the diagrams and answering questions about them. For example, *Which diagram has a wheel labelled on it?*

Get a Move On! by Anita Ganeri in the *Body Books* series (Evans Brothers) has labelled diagrams in it. *Me and My Body* by Rosie McCormick in the *Fun Finding Out* series is also suitable for this age group.

1: 2: T17: to use terms 'fiction' and 'non-fiction', noting some of their differing features, e.g. layout, titles, contents page, use of pictures, labelled diagrams

1: 2: T22: to write labels for drawings and diagrams, e.g. growing beans, parts of the body

1: 2: T24: to write simple questions, e.g. as part of interactive display (*'How many…?', 'Where is your house…?'*)

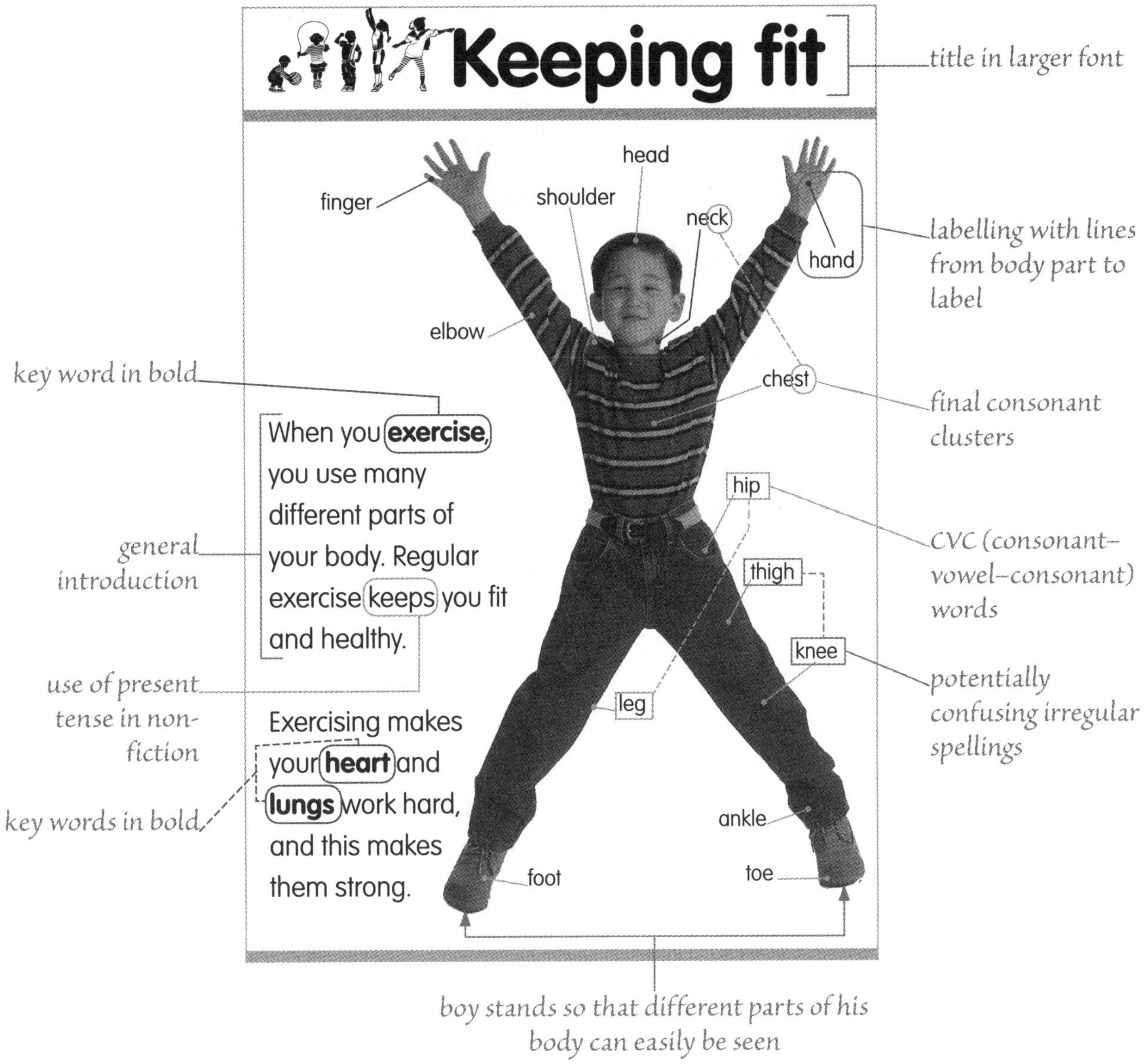

1: 2: T25: to assemble information from own experience, e.g. food, pets; to use simple sentences to describe, based on examples from reading; to write simple non-chronological reports; and to organise in lists, separate pages, charts

1: 2: W3: to discriminate, read and spell words with initial consonant clusters, e.g. *bl, cr, tr, str* – Appendix List 3

1: 2: W10: to gather new words from reading and shared experiences and to make collections of personal interest or significant words and words linked to particular topics

Hearing

by Mandy Suhr

P 138

Background

Hearing, from which this text is taken, is one of the titles in *The Senses* series that has been especially written and designed for young readers. The extract is a simple, factual text which explores our sense of hearing by presenting information in everyday language to which children will relate.

This extract is written in the form of a non-chronological report and will provide a useful starting point for discussion during shared reading. The simple statements are written in the second person, which is not typical of this type of report. However, the author uses this more personal style to appeal directly to the reader. More typical characteristics of non-chronological reports are also present: a clear opening sentence that explains and introduces the topic; simple factual statements that outline the qualities, parts and functions of the ears; definitions and explanations. This extract also provides opportunities to examine the differences between fact and fiction.

Shared reading and discussing the text

- Remind the children about the purpose of a non-chronological report. (Reports can give us scientific or factual information about a range of topics, for example plants, animals and places.) Explain to the children that this report is about one of the five senses: hearing. Identify the other senses.
- Read the extract to the children, pausing to discuss each new piece of information.
- Now read the text again and ask the children to read with you. Stop at the end of each sentence and point out the number of facts contained in each, for example the third sentence in the extract tells us two things about the outer ear: it catches sounds and sends the sounds down a hole in your ear.
- Read the sentences about the ear-drum together. Show the children a music drum and talk about how the skin is stretched across the frame/outer part of the drum. Place some shreds of coloured tissue paper on the surface of the drum and ask the children to observe what happens to these when the drum is hit and the sound vibrates the skin. Explain that when sounds travel through the air and reaches our ears it causes our ear-drums to vibrate. This sends a message to our brain to tell us to try to identify the sound. The author of the extract avoids using technical vocabulary in her explanations – however, words such as *vibrations* and *membrane* could be introduced to children at this point to extend their vocabulary.

Activities

- Work in small groups with the children to write facts about hearing, such as *Sounds travel through...* Check that sentences begin with a capital letter and end with a full stop.
- Take the children into the playground and conduct an experiment to find out if a sound is more difficult to hear when the listener moves further away from the person/object making the sound (ensure this is a 'fair test'). Return to the classroom and ask the children to draw a diagram with labels to report on the experiment.
- Ask the children to describe and identify the sounds made by playing different percussion instruments behind a screen. Make a list of the descriptive words generated. Encourage the children to explain how the sound was produced. Talk about soft and loud sounds.
- Write a 'sound' poem about classroom sounds or rainy day sounds, for example.

Extension/further reading

Make string telephones and ask the children to work in pairs to interview each other about how they made their telephones and how sound travels.

Talk about people who have hearing difficulties. Describe how sign language is another form of communication that some deaf people use.

Further reading includes *Hearing Sounds* by Sally Hewitt in *It's Science!* (Franklin Watts).

1: 2: T17: to use terms 'fiction' and 'non-fiction', noting some of their differing features, e.g. layout, titles, contents page, use of pictures, labelled diagrams

Hearing

illustration to support text

Sounds travel through the air but you can't see them.

opening explains topic clearly; differs from a story (for example, 'Once upon a time…')

You use your ears to hear them.

written in 2nd person; report is factual but draws reader in by making it sound as though author is talking directly to you

The outer part of your ear catches the sounds and sends them down a hole. This hole leads to a tunnel that goes right inside your ear.

outlines what happens

simple factual statements

At the end of the tunnel there is a thin bit of skin. This is stretched tight across the end of the tunnel, just like the skin on the top of a drum.

avoids using technical vocabulary

shows functions of ear

This is called your ear-drum.

1: 2: T18: to read non-fiction books and understand that the reader doesn't need to go from start to finish but selects according to what is needed

1: 2: T25: to assemble information from own experience, e.g. food, pets; to use simple sentences to describe, based on examples from reading; to write simple non-chronological reports; and to organise in lists, separate pages, charts

Weather: rain

by Jillian Powell

P 139

Background

This extract is from *Rain and Us*, one of a series of four titles about the weather that offers clear, concise information. You will be able to use it as a starting point to help children learn about the differences between fact and fiction. It will also allow you to introduce children to some of the textual and linguistic features that are characteristic of non-chronological reports, such as the use of sub-headings to help organise information, the use of the present tense and the inclusion of subject-specific vocabulary.

Shared reading and discussing the text

- Before reading the extract, ask the children to tell you about the different sorts of weather they have experienced in the last few days. What sorts of weather do they like/dislike?
- Identify and read the title of the extract and then read the sub-headings. Explain the difference between these and talk about how the author uses different devices to organise the text – questions in sub-headings, paragraph headings, words in bold or different fonts, and so on. Point out how the information is presented and grouped together on the page.
- Read half of the extract to the children and ask them to tell you what sort of writing it is. (Is it a story, a poem, a list? Is it giving us information? Is it fact or fiction?)
- Read the rest of the extract and explain that the information in the text is part of a factual report about rain. Talk about how information in this sort of report does not need to be read in order, from cover to cover like a story. The information is organised into short sections and is presented in a non-chronological way so that the reader can choose which part to find out about first. It is written in the present tense. For example, in *They fall as balls of ice*, the author is describing how hailstones are formed and does not need to say whether it happened yesterday or today or may happen tomorrow.
- Discuss the meaning of any unfamiliar words, such as *deserts*, *hailstones* and *layers*.

Activities

- Cut up enlarged copies of the extract into separate phrases and give each child a sentence to reassemble. Once the children have become familiar with the facts in this way, give them the first half of a sentence and ask them to finish the sentence. They can do this either in a written format or orally in small groups.
- Compare this extract to the poem 'Weather' by Eve Merriam (see page 58). Talk about the differences in the type of information given and how it is organised. Discuss the way in which 'Weather' is quite difficult to read; the poet wants you to have fun pronouncing the tongue-twisters and guessing at the meanings of made-up words; and how the language and imagery help us to imagine it is raining. In the information text here, however, the author tries to write simple sentences with clear explanations and definitions to help us make sense of the facts. Read out lines from each text to illustrate these points.
- Work in guided groups and collect 'rain' words, starting with words from the extract, for example *raindrops, drizzle, clouds*, and adding to them – *mist, droplets, puddles...* Use a dictionary and a thesaurus to support this task. Then encourage the children to think of imagery and idiomatic phrases related to rainy weather, such as *It's raining cats and dogs*. In this way you will be able to build up a shared understanding of the topic and begin to eradicate children's errors and misconceptions.

Extension/further reading

Write a weather report about the next rainy day you have. Invite the children to use the technical vocabulary they have learned to be precise about the type of rain they observed.

Make a rain diary. Create a chart and keep a pictorial record of the different sorts of rain experienced over a two-week period. Design a key with simple definitions to match the pictures.

Another information book about the weather is *Sun and Us* by Jillian Powell (Belitha Press).

1: 2: T19: to predict what a given book might be about from a brief look at both front and back covers, including blurb, title, illustration; to discuss what it might tell in advance of reading and check to see if it does

1: 2: T22: to write labels for drawings and diagrams, e.g. growing beans, parts of the body

Weather: rain

What is rain?
Rain is water that falls from the sky as raindrops. Some parts of the world may have rain all year round. **Deserts** have little or no rain.

Clouds, hail and fog
If raindrops travel high up in the clouds where it is very cold, they freeze. They fall as balls of ice called **hailstones.** If you cut a hailstone in half you can see the layers of ice.

Rain fact
Light rain made up of small raindrops is called drizzle.

information is organised and grouped together in different sections

present tense

sub-headings in bold

fact

definition of rain

rain words

technical vocabulary

simple sentence, giving us information

rain word

1: 2: T23: to produce extended captions, e.g. to explain paintings in wall displays or to describe artefacts

1: 2: T25: to assemble information from own experience, e.g. food, pets; to use simple sentences to describe, based on examples from reading; to write simple non-chronological reports; and to organise in lists, separate pages, charts

A minibeast

by Barbara Taylor

P 140

Background

This non-chronological report about a minibeast is informative yet concise and introduces children to some subject-specific terminology. It is written in the first person – this is not a typical feature of non-chronological reports, but it helps to draw the reader into the minibeast's world.

Shared reading and discussing the text

- Before introducing the extract, display a selection of books about minibeasts. Include a range of text types, both fiction and non-fiction. Ask the children to choose the texts that will help them to find out facts about minibeasts. Discuss the differences between the fact and fiction books you have on display.
- Discuss the title of the extract and talk about the layout of the text, for example the title is in bigger print and bold type, the text is split up into three parts (paragraphs) and there is a photograph on the page. Ask the children if they know what sort of creature a cricket is. Has anyone seen a cricket before?
- Read the text, pausing to talk about the meaning of any unfamiliar words, for example *collar, protects* and *antennae*. Explain that authors use this sort of technical vocabulary to help them describe something in a precise and accurate way.
- Ask the children to tell a friend about one thing they have found out about crickets. Ask for feedback from some children. Check their statements by referring to the text to locate the evidence, circling or highlighting relevant parts of the text.
- Invite the children to read the text with you this time. Ask the children to tell you who the *I* is in the text. Who is telling us this information? Talk about the personal style, from the viewpoint of the cricket.
- Make a list of the different sorts of information given about the cricket. Categorise these for children as you write them on the board, for example appearance, movement, functions of body parts, senses, food.
- Ask the children to think of one more thing they would like to find out about crickets. Agree on one question and write it on the board, for example *Where do crickets live?*

Activities

- Give the children some sentences cut out from an enlarged copy of the text. Work with small groups to think of new sub-headings to help to clarify each factual statement. Write these down on separate strips of paper. Match the sentences with the sub-headings, for example <u>Senses</u> – *I see well with my big eyes.* <u>*Eating*</u> – *My biting jaws cut and grind up my food.*
- Ask the children to work in pairs or small groups to complete a KWL grid about another minibeast, for example a snail:
  - What do they already *know* about snails? (For example, *Snails carry a shell on their back.*)
  - *What* would they like to find out? (For example, *What is a snail's shell for?*)
  - What have they *learned* about snails?

The children can then use this information to write non-chronological reports about snails.

- Create a class minibeast book comprising the children's written reports about other creatures found in the school grounds during a minibeast hunt. Use the structure of the extract as a scaffold (*Habitat* is an additional heading). Encourage the children to add a drawing.

Type of minibeast	**Picture**
Appearance:	
Functions of body parts:	
Senses:	
Habitat:	
Food:	

Extension/further reading

In the Tall, Tall Grass by Denise Fleming (Red Fox) is a nature book that is ideal for Year 1 children.

1: 2: T17: to use terms 'fiction' and 'non-fiction', noting some of their differing features, e.g. layout, titles, contents page, use of pictures, labelled diagrams

1: 2: T18: to read non-fiction books and understand that the reader doesn't need to go from start to finish but selects according to what is needed

A MINIBEAST

I am a jumping cricket.

1 My enormous back legs have strong muscles that help me jump a long way. I have a hard collar behind my head that protects the front part of my body.

2 I see well with my big eyes. My front legs can sense sounds.

3 I touch and smell things with my long antennae. My biting jaws cut and grind up my food.

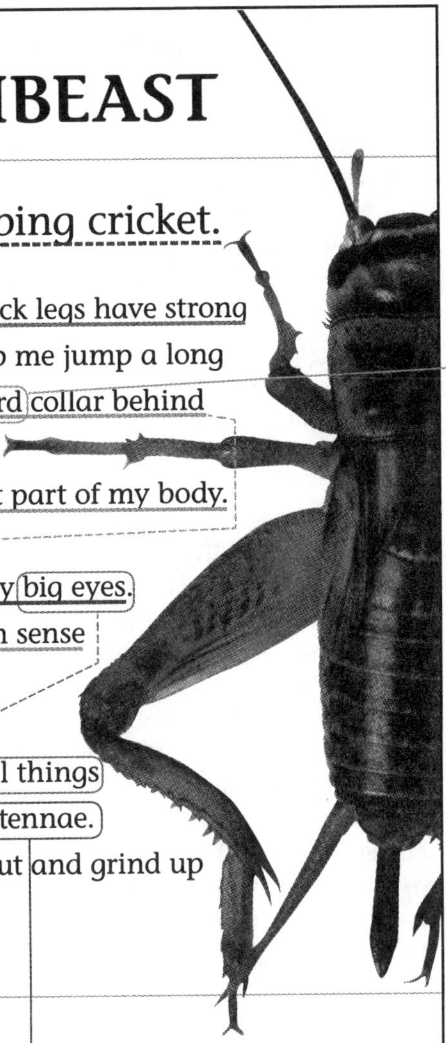

bold sub-heading

text is split into 3 parts (paragraphs) to organise information

appearance

written in 1st person (from cricket's point of view)

simple sentences written in present tense

functions of body parts

senses

descriptive language used to make information clear and precise

for food

technical vocabulary

1: 2: T21: to understand the purpose of contents pages and indexes and to begin to locate information by page numbers and words by initial letter

1: 2: T22: to write labels for drawings and diagrams, e.g. growing beans, parts of the body

1: 2: T25: to assemble information from own experience, e.g. food, pets; to use simple sentences to describe, based on examples from reading; to write simple non-chronological reports; and to organise in lists, separate pages, charts

Duckling

by Angela Royston

P 141

Background

This extract is taken from *Baby Animals*, in the *Eye Openers* series of photographic information books for young children. Each double-page spread in the book is devoted to one type of baby animal and follows a common format. This extract about ducklings is a simple text, written in the present tense which effectively demonstrates how non-chronological reports document, organise and display information. Consequently, once children have become immersed in the features of this genre, by sharing the extract with you, they will be able to apply and consolidate their skills when reading the rest of the text or similar books independently.

Shared reading and discussing the text

- Before reading the extract, talk about the type of text it is and the layout on the page – it is non-fiction, it contains factual information, it includes photographs.
- Explain that this text is going to tell us about baby ducks. These are called ducklings. (You could show the children a photograph of an adult duck at this point.) Ask the children if they have ever seen a duckling before. What other baby animals have they seen, for example kittens or puppies?
- Read the text to the children, pausing to discuss the meaning of unfamiliar words, such as *hatch* and *down*. Involve the children in looking up the meanings of these words and agree a definition that can be written on the board.
- Talk about what we have learned after engaging with this text. Ask the children if they were surprised by any of the facts they have found out about ducklings. You could model this to encourage the children to be curious about the text and to become actively involved in constructing meaning and assimilating new information, for example *I was surprised to learn that ducklings can walk and follow their mother as soon as they have been born. Human babies can't do that can they?*

Activities

- Ask the children to work in pairs to answer one of the following questions about the text:
  - What does *hatch* mean?
  - What do ducklings look like when they are one day old?
  - How are they cared for?
  - Where do they find food?
  - Which part of a duckling's body is called the beak?
  - What do ducklings' feet look like?
  - What is *down*?
  - What happens to the duckling's soft down after a few weeks?

This could be done as a written or as an oral task. Once the children have rehearsed their answer and referred to the text to check it, they can feed back to the rest of the class. They will need reminding about how to structure sentences in response to these questions. You could model this by writing a sentence with children in small groups in order to highlight the use of the present tense, a formal style, and generic participants, for example the text refers to *ducklings* rather than *Daphne the duckling*.

- Use this text as a model to help children write their own non-chronological report about another baby animal. Provide them with a writing frame to scaffold their report. This could include prompts such as *How is the baby animal born? What does the animal look like? What does the animal eat? How does the animal move? Where does this animal live?* (Habitat). *How does the animal's appearance change over time?*
- Create a class display complete with labelled diagrams, a title, sub-headings and captions.

Extension/further reading

Devise a matching game that involves pairing up the name of a baby animal with its adult name, *duckling/duck; piglet/pig*, and so on.

Other titles in this series are *Farm Animals, Pets* and *Night-time Animals* (Atheneum). *Five Little Ducks* by Ian Beck (Orchard Books) is a fiction book that children will enjoy.

1: 2: T17: to use terms 'fiction' and 'non-fiction', noting some of their differing features, e.g. layout, titles, contents page, use of pictures, labelled diagrams

1: 2: T22: to write labels for drawings and diagrams, e.g. growing beans, parts of the body

headings and labelled photographs are features of non-fiction texts

Duckling

unfamiliar word — hatch

present tense — follow

moves from general to specific

Ducklings hatch from eggs. Soon after hatching, they follow the mother duck to the pond to find food.

These ducklings are just one day old. In a few weeks they will lose their soft down and grow feathers.

tells us what the ducklings are like

1: 2: T24: to write simple questions, e.g. as part of interactive display (*'How many…?', 'Where is your house…?'*)

1: 2: T25: to assemble information from own experience, e.g. food, pets; to use simple sentences to describe, based on examples from reading; to write simple non-chronological reports; and to organise in lists, separate pages, charts

Healthy eating

P 142

Background

This non-chronological report will provide a useful starting point for a class topic on food and health. The text begins with a clear introductory sentence and goes on to define the subject and to classify information under sub-headings. This information is supported and extended through the use of illustrations. The report addresses the reader directly and attempts to relate information to children's own experiences (for example, *When you run about at playtime...*).

Shared reading and discussing the text

- Before reading the text, ask the children to talk about different types of food they like to eat. Write the foods on the board, drawing a simple picture to accompany each word. Discuss which ones are particularly good for us because they keep us healthy. This will indicate how much the children already know about the topic.
- Ask the children to help you to complete the first two columns of a KWL grid:

1. Know What do we think we know about healthy eating?	**2. What** What would we like to find out about healthy eating?	**3. Learned** What have we learned in answer to our questions?

- Explain that you are going to start researching this topic by reading a short report about healthy eating. Now read the text, pausing to talk about the meaning of unfamiliar words. Make a list of these (for example, *protein, balanced diet, energy, carbohydrates*).
- Look at the way the extract is presented. Highlight the title and sub-headings and point out that the pictures are used to give us more information. Ask the children to identify a question in the text. Talk about the use of question marks and question words (for example, *which*). Explain that this type of writing (a non-chronological report) aims to describe specific things and presents us with information. Questions are sometimes included to prompt us to think about things.
- Read the text again and encourage the children to join in this time (perhaps some of the KWL questions will be answered as you read). Ask the children to look at the original brainstorm list on the board and to identify foods under the headings found in the text here (protein foods and carbohydrates). Use the illustrations to help the children compare the lists. Check to see if any of the foods on the list are 'sugary' foods. Talk about how we need to moderate our intake of these foods in order to maintain a balanced diet and stay healthy.

Activities

- Ask the children to suggest other sources of information about healthy eating. Make a list of the places/people/texts that might provide them with more information, such as family members, the school cook, the Internet, a library, a supermarket. (Try to implement some research using these sources.)
- Work with small groups of children to make a glossary explaining the unfamiliar, technical vocabulary in the text.
- Involve the children in making their own healthy eating books with simple, factual sentences and labelled illustrations.
- At the end of the topic/period of research, ask the children to complete the last column of the KWL grid. This could be done during shared writing, guided writing or independently.

Extension/further reading

Ask the children to use their own books to help them explain the importance of eating healthily to small groups of children in the reception or nursery class. The children could share fruit together, look at the books and talk about how they researched the topic.

Further reading includes the story *Handa's Surprise* by Eileen Browne (Walker Books) and the non-fiction book *I Eat Fruit!* by Hannah Tofts (Zero to Ten).

1: 2: T17: to use terms 'fiction' and 'non-fiction', noting some of their differing features, e.g. layout, titles, contents page, use of pictures, labelled diagrams

Healthy eating

You need food to help your body grow and to give you energy. Different sorts of food help to keep you healthy. That is why it is important to eat a balanced diet. This means that you should eat different types of food every day so that you get all the nutrients your body needs.

Different foods help your body in different ways.

Growth and repair

Protein foods help you to grow by feeding your muscles, skin and bones.

Which of these foods do you like to eat? You should eat some of these foods every day as proteins also help your body to repair itself when it gets injured.

Food for energy

You can help to give your body energy by eating foods that contain carbohydrates.

Carbohydrates can be found in these foods.

When you run about at playtime and exercise in PE lessons you use up lots of energy. You even use energy when you are asleep!

Carbohydrates can also be found in sugary foods such as jam, cakes and chocolate.

Do you think these foods can help you to stay healthy?

heading (usually identifies topic specifically)

introductory sentence

clear opening paragraph

images to support text and provide more information

subject-specific terminology

factual sentences that describe and explain specific things

question to prompt discussion

capital letter and full stop in sentence

sub-heading used to group information and to organise text

question to draw reader in and to introduce more information

1: 2: T22: to write labels for drawings and diagrams, e.g. growing beans, parts of the body

1: 2: T25: to assemble information from own experience, e.g. food, pets; to use simple sentences to describe, based on examples from reading; to write simple non-chronological reports; and to organise in lists, separate pages, charts

UFO Diary

by Satoshi Kitamura

P 143

Background

UFO Diary is a story of an alien who takes a wrong turning in space and lands on the planet Earth. The alien spots a 'creature', a small boy, who stares in amazement as the alien spaceship lands. The two become friends and the boy gets a ride in the spaceship. The boy gives him a present from Earth, a buttercup from the field, and the alien promises to plant it.

This story is appealing not only because of the idea of a boy meeting an alien and riding in space, but also because of the bond that forms between two creatures from totally different worlds. It also makes a good introduction to the genre of fantasy.

Shared reading and discussing the text

- Look at the text – a scan of the front and back covers of the book. Read the title and discuss the term *UFO*. Link this with the object flying in the sky in the picture and explain that *UFO* stands for 'unidentified flying object'. Ensure that the children know what a diary is used for, then paraphrase the title – for example, *the daily events of a flying saucer.*
- Ask the children if flying saucers really do exist and lead this into a discussion about 'fantasy'.
- Look at the back cover and explain that the writing is called the *blurb*. Read the text to the children and talk about its purpose: to give a 'taste' of what is in the book and to persuade readers to read it.
- Now predict the story, using the illustration, and discuss what the children can see. Go back to the title – does it give good clues to the story? Contrast it with *A diary of a small boy*, for example, which would give very few clues.
- Give the children a synopsis of the story (see above) or, if you have a copy of the book, read the whole story to them. How does this compare to their own predictions?
- Focusing on the first three lines of text in the blurb, ask the children how they know this is a sentence. Contrast it with a short sentence, for example *An alien lands on Earth.* Explain that sentences vary in length and do not always finish at the end of a line in a book.

Activities

- Look carefully at the words contained in the blurb and tell the children that they are going to make a 'fantasy word wall' of words from fantasy stories. Ask them to read the extract in pairs and to put a ring around strange words. Include these words in the word wall.
- Let the children create their own fantasy book cover containing a title, illustration and blurb. Encourage pairs to brainstorm good titles, using vocabulary from the fantasy word wall.
- Brainstorm what it would be like to ride in a spaceship. Model planning a story, with headings of *What it looked like; What it felt like; What it sounded like*, and so on. Now ask the children to add suitable words under each heading. More able children could write sentences under the headings, to form their own little stories. Less able children could be given key words to help them or sentences starters, for example *In the spaceship it felt... I could see...*

Extension/further reading

Play 'Guess my present' – the children take it in turns to describe a suitable present for an alien, the other children guessing what the present is.

The boy and the alien are best friends. In circle time, ask the children to describe a best friend – *A best friend needs to be...* Then focus on *It is good to be different:* one child sits in the centre of the circle and decides on different categories to determine how others swap places, for example *Everyone with brown hair change places.*

Other stories about fantasy worlds include *The Brave Little Grork* by Kathryn Cave (Hodder Children's Books), *But Martin!* by June Counsel (Faber & Faber), *Dr Xargle's Book of Earthlets* (and others in the series) by Jeanne Willis (Andersen Press) and *Where the Wild Things Are* by Maurice Sendak (Red Fox).

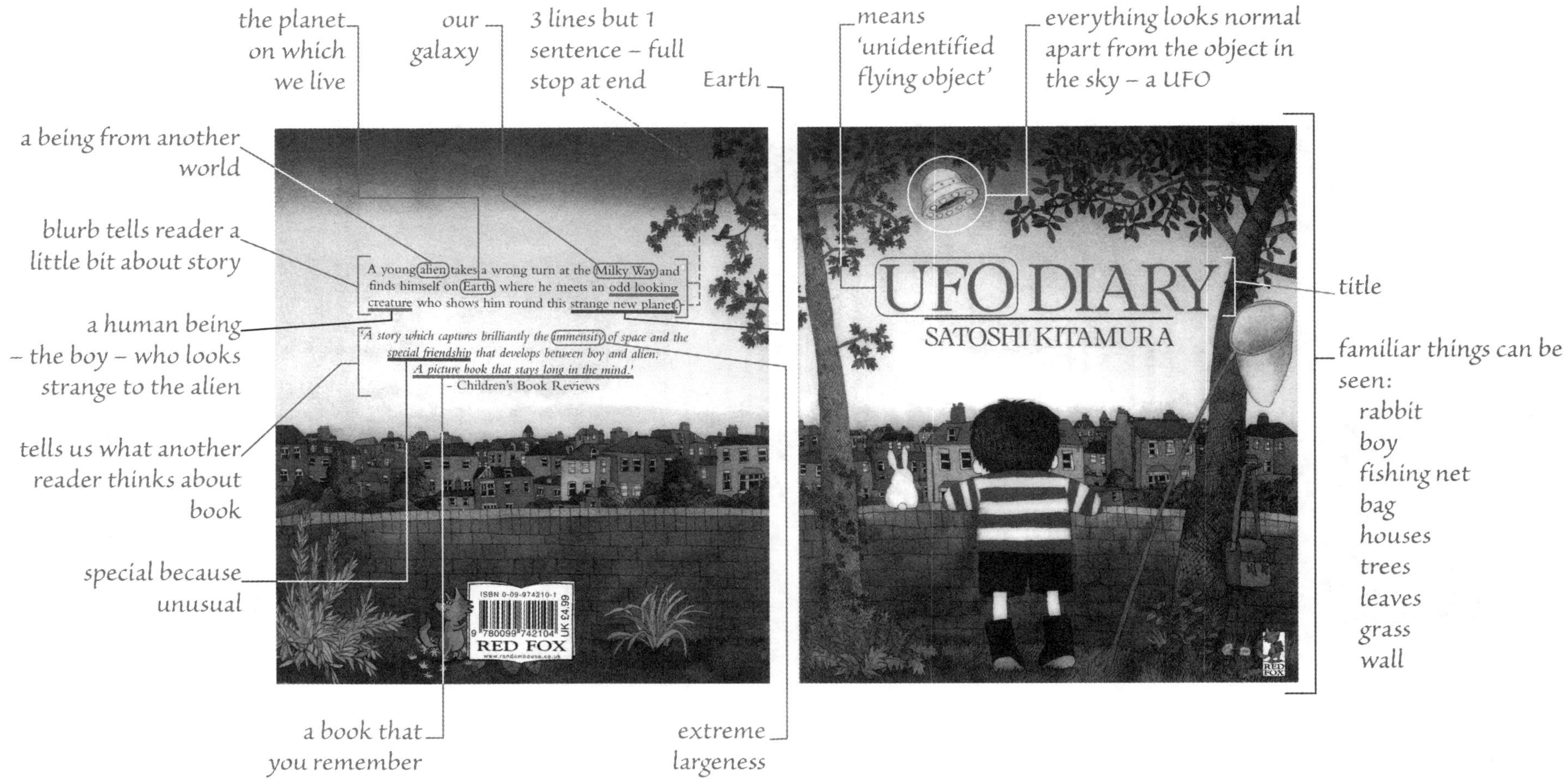

1: 3: T7: to use titles, cover pages and 'blurbs' to predict the content of unfamiliar stories

1: 3: S6: through reading and writing, to reinforce knowledge of term 'sentence' from previous terms

1: 3: W8: new words from reading and shared experiences, and to make collections of personal interest or significant words and words linked to particular topics

Through the Magic Mirror by Anthony Browne

P 144

Background

This is a story of a boy in a normal home setting who is bored. He spots the mirror upstairs and walks right through it. The rest of the story shows how even though things seem partially normal, everyday scenes are very different. In the end, the boy returns through the mirror and goes to have his tea. The extract illustrates the power of the visual image and can be used as an excellent basis for discussion, and for work on comparing and transforming everyday settings into fantasy ones.

Shared reading and discussing the text

- Read the text, with the children using an enlarged copy. Discuss the fact that the words do not give us much information about what is going on and that the pictures give vital clues.
- Brainstorm with the children everything they can see in the illustration. Now discuss what is wrong with it, for example in the second half there is a large goldfish in the window, with its tail in front of its head.
- Discuss what is happening in the story and provide some background (see above). If you have a copy of the book, read the whole text to the children. Talk about whether they ever play in imaginary worlds.
- Look at the word *street* together. Ask the children how many phonemes they can hear (five) and tell them to put 'phoneme buttons' (coloured dots) under each phoneme. Now ask the children for any words that share the same end sound. Write a list on the board, for example *meet, feet, sleet.* Use this opportunity to discuss different spellings of words that share the same sound, for example *meat, heat, beat*, and provide lists of words for display.
- Look again at the text and highlight common irregular words, such as *like* and *was.* Discuss how some words have 'strange' spellings and are not written as they sound. Take a word at a time and talk about ways in which the spellings can be remembered. For example, write *was* on the board and highlight the tricky part of the word – *as.* Talk about how you can remember it, such as saying the word as it is written: *w-a-s.* Use a similar procedure with other common irregular words.

Activities

- Ask pairs of children to find as many strange things as possible in the illustration. Provide them with a two-columned chart for comparing the everyday and fantasy settings – that is, what they would normally expect to see in the street with what they see in the picture.
- Model writing a description of an everyday setting with a fantastic element, for example a classroom with real animals in a toy Noah's ark, a classroom with ordinary objects in strange places, such as the teacher's desk high on the wall and the whiteboard on the floor. Follow this with asking the children to write their own description of a fantasy-world setting. Give them a page on which you have drawn a box surrounded by suitable words, for example familiar words such as *desk, chair, table*, and unexpected words for the context, such as *lion, tiger, elephant.* Ask the children to draw their setting in the box and to write a sentence underneath it to describe the 'story' in their picture.
- Following whole-class work, ask the children to work on common spelling patterns for the long vowel sound *ee* as in *street* by collecting similar words from their reading to add to words on display.
- Reinforce spelling common irregular words (for example, *like, was*) by asking the children to track them in the text and to practise using mnemonics, for example *we are silly* for *was.*

Extension/further reading

Use the story as a stimulus for PSHE and citizenship work on feelings. Discuss how familiar things make us feel secure and strange or unusual things can make us frightened.

Changes (Walker Books) is a story by Anthony Browne in which objects start to change in appearance as a boy waits at home for the arrival of a new baby sister.

Through the Magic Mirror

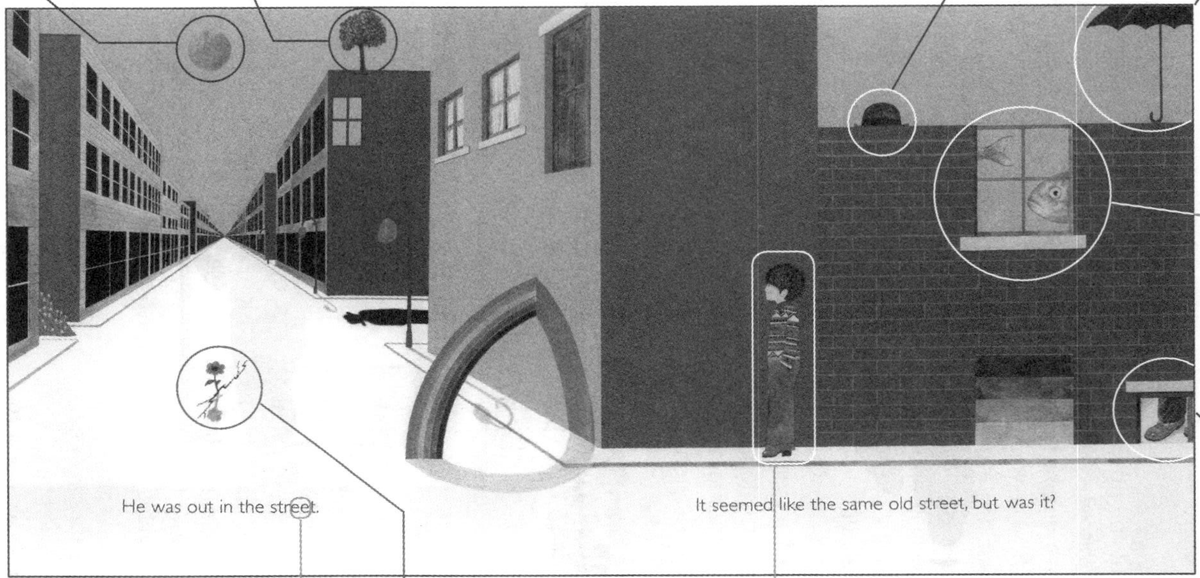

1: 3: T8: to compare and contrast stories with a variety of settings, e.g. space, imaginary lands, animal homes

1: 3: T14: to write stories using simple settings, e.g. based on previous reading

1: 3: W1: the common spelling pattern for the long vowel phoneme *ee*:
- to identify phonemes in speech and writing
- to blend phonemes for reading
- to segment words into phonemes for spelling

1: 3: W7: to spell common irregular words from Appendix List 1

Falling Angels by Colin Thompson

P 145

Background

This is an allegorical tale about the power of literature. It tells of Sally, who discovers when she is a baby that she can fly to distant lands she has only seen in books and how her mother thinks she just has a vivid imagination. Sally finds out that she shares the same gift with her grandmother who could also once fly, and Sally discovers from her that she has learned to see the world not just with her eyes, but with her heart. Sally brings her amazing treasures from exotic places and finally takes her grandmother flying with her. Dreaming of her favourite places, Grandmother takes her last breath, but Sally goes on to teach her own children and grandchildren to 'fly'.

This book has a strong fantasy element and can be used for comparing and writing about imaginary settings. The extract is from the beginning of the story, showing some of the fantastic and magical places Sally visits and the orchid she takes to her grandmother.

Shared reading and discussing the text

- Begin by talking about the book with the children, and put the extract into context by providing some background (see above). Ask the children if they would like to fly to wonderful places, or if they can imagine they could by reading about them. Now read the text to the children. Talk about the type of book (fantasy) and whether they think Sally can really fly. Explain that this is all about the power of the imagination and how stories can help.
- Discuss the special relationship Sally has with her grandmother. Ask the children to talk in pairs about a person who is special to them.
- Re-read the extract, this time with it enlarged, and ask the children to join in. Ask them to discuss with a partner whether they like books that contain magical and fantastic places, and to report back to the class with reasons why they do or do not like fantasy settings.
- Now look at some of the words in the extract and talk about the long vowel sounds in the words, for example *oa* in *floated*. Brainstorm a range of similar words, for example *boat*, and ensure the children can segment the words into the individual phonemes. Then move on to words with the long vowel phoneme *oo*, as in the words *too, room* and *afternoon* from the extract.

Activities

- Talk about the settings described in the extract (Sally's house and neighbourhood; faraway lands; and the rainforest in Africa). Ask the children to choose one of the settings, and then to illustrate it and write a sentence to describe it. Compare and display the children's contrasting settings.
- Discuss why Sally brought back an orchid, ensuring that the children understand that this is an exotic plant from a far-off land. Ask them to draw and write a description of a precious object collected from an imaginary journey, for example a special shell.
- Use the journey portrayed in the extract to model a story map to an imaginary place. Provide plenty of opportunities for the children to talk about different places they could visit on their own imaginary travels and then ask them to draw a story map showing their journey. More able children could write a story about travelling to an imaginary world, using their story map as a basis. Less able children could tell their story orally.

Extension/further reading

If you have a copy of the book, examine carefully the illustrations, for example strange stairways and bridges, golden eggs, wizard's hats and books with legs. Some children may make links to films they have seen such as *Harry Potter and the Philosopher's Stone*.

Other journey stories include *We're Going on a Bear Hunt* by Michael Rosen (Walker Books), *Whatever Next!* by Jill Murphy (Macmillan Children's Books), *Mr Gumpy's Outing* by John Burningham (Red Fox). These books also provide opportunities to contrast different settings.

1: 3: T8: to compare and contrast stories with a variety of settings, e.g. space, imaginary lands, animal homes

1: 3: T4: to read with sufficient concentration to complete a text, and to identify preferences and give reasons

Falling Angels

The first time Sally flew was before she could even crawl. As her parents slept, she floated above them, too young to speak, too young to think in words.

The first time Sally saw someone else flying, she was seven. Her mother was sleeping in the warm summer afternoon. Beside her in the grass her baby brother Peter curled up in her shadow. As Sally floated over the garden, she saw the baby stretch out and rise into the air.

Maybe it's just us, she thought, something special about our family.

As the years passed, Sally flew to wild and wonderful places, distant lands she had only seen in books. And in the afternoons she sat by her grandmother's bed and told her about everything she'd seen.

"You and your silly stories," said her mother. "It's time you came down to earth."

"They're not stories," said Sally when her mother had left the room.

Her grandmother just smiled.

I'll prove it, said Sally to herself, and the next morning, while everyone was still asleep, she flew into the heart of Africa. She watched the sun creep over the horizon and wake up the world for another day. She flew into the deepest part of the rainforest and in the branches of a great firewheel tree she found a beautiful orchid, which she took back to her grandmother.

fantasy story – how can a human being fly?

familiar setting of home

long vowel sound 'oa'

long vowel sound 'oo'

normal situation – mother and baby brother in the garden – which then changes

clue to the story

Sally's mother doesn't believe her

reader picks up that grandmother thinks differently from mother

setting

exotic plant

orchid taken as gift for her grandmother but also to give proof of her travels

1: 3: W1: the common spelling patterns for each of the long vowel phonemes: *oa, oo* (long as in *moon*) Appendix List 3:

- to identify phonemes in speech and writing
- to blend phonemes for reading
- to segment words into phonemes for spelling

The Brave Little Grork by Kathryn Cave

P 146

Background

This extract is from a story about two imaginary characters – a 'grork' and a 'greep'. It tells of a visit to the woods and how the grork spends ages preparing what to take in order to help to overcome his fears. The greep encourages him with *brave thoughts*, the grork runs in fear when he gets to a haunted tree and finally runs into what he thinks is a monster – a *turple*. When he opens his eyes he sees it is Flurp, a friend. The story ends with the three of them singing on their way home.

This text is a good example of fantasy, with strange creatures as the characters. It is taken from the climax of the story when the grork and greep are in the wood and run for their lives because of a strange noise. Using a cliffhanger like this can stimulate children's interest and provide material for prediction work. The strong theme of being scared is also one with which children can easily identify.

Shared reading and discussing the text

- Introduce the story to the children, first showing them the pictures of the main characters, the grork and greep. Talk about their strange characters and names, but also make sure the children understand their different personalities – that is, grorks are very shy and easily frightened and greeps are quite the opposite.
- Now read the extract with the children, with plenty of expression to highlight the build up of tension brought about by the *haunted tree* and *the old crow who'd been struck by lightning*, and exaggerate the word *cree-ee-eaked!* Ensure that you emphasise the cliffhanger of *'Run for your life.'* Ask the children what they think will happen next.
- Talk about friendships and how the grork and greep are good friends and help each other, for example discussing the benefits of *thinking brave thoughts*. Encourage the children to tell you about times when they have been frightened; you could share an example with them of something that has frightened you.
- Now look closely at the extract and explain that stories tell us about things that happened in the past and that words ending in *ed* usually show that something has already happened. Look for examples in the text – *wanted, waited* – and highlight them. Contrast this with how the words would be written in the present – *want* and *wait*.

Activities

- Ask the children to talk in pairs about a range of possible endings. Model writing an ending and then ask the children to rehearse orally a sentence for an ending before writing it down. Contrast the children's versions with the author's ending (see above).
- Focusing on the grork and the greep, suggest that the children look carefully at the illustrations of them and write a description of their characters. Provide them with key words such as *shy, frightened, bold* and so on.
- This extract contains a significant incident in the story. Ask the children to role-play what happened in the wood by the haunted tree.
- Now take the incident the children have acted out and brainstorm suitable phrases that could create a similarly 'scary' scene, such as *owls hoot, the wind whistles...* Ask the children to find corresponding verbs for a list of nouns you provide (*lightning, hail, birds, cats,* and so on). More able children could use these as a basis for a story involving imaginary characters who have strange names and frightening adventures. Less able children could draw their own imaginary characters for display.

Extension/further reading

Link this text to stories and poems about fears (and who or what helps us to overcome them), such as *The Bear Under the Stairs* by Helen Cooper (Picture Corgi), *The Park in the Dark* and *Can't you Sleep, Little Bear?* by Martin Waddell (Walker Books), the poems 'In the Dark' by Jane Pridmore and 'The Bogus-Boo' by James Reeves from *A First Poetry Book* compiled by John Foster (OUP).

1: 3: T5: to retell stories, to give the main points in sequence and to pick out significant incidents

strange names in a fantasy story

'ed' endings to show that the story happened in the past

The Brave Little Grork

One day the greep wanted to go to the wood. He waited patiently while the grork got ready. This took a long time.

"Thinking brave thoughts works," he said, very excited. "It really does."

"It works for me too," the greep said.

But suddenly, there they were by the haunted tree. The grork had heard that an old crow who'd been struck by lightning swooped down from its branches on stormy nights.

The grork felt small and frightened. Before he could think brave thoughts, the wind blew and the branches

cree-ee-eaked!

"Run," cried the grork.
"Run for your life."

This is a **grork**.
Grorks are shy and easily frightened.

This is a **greep**.
Greeps are not shy and they hardly ever get frightened.

scary setting – haunted tree in the wood

characters from fantasy world (they are not real); each type of character has its own appearance and personality

this lets us know he is scared but pretending to be brave as he gives advice to greep

climax of story

mysterious tale about the crow helps to build tension

large bird, black in colour

word in bold larger type for emphasis

cliffhanger – what will happen next?

1: 3: T14: to write stories using simple settings, e.g. based on previous reading

1: 3: W6: to investigate and learn spellings of verbs with 'ed' (past tense) endings

Porwigles

by Julie Holder

P 147

Background

This poem takes a structure reminiscent of 'Ten Green Bottles' or 'Five Little Ducks' and presents an alternative humorous version. It lends itself to reading aloud with expression, with varying volume and tone at appropriate points. As the poet explains, *porwigle* is an old English name for a tadpole.

Shared reading and discussing the text

- First explain what a porwigle is, telling the children that it is an old-fashioned name; use examples of other words that have changed over time such as *wireless*, now *radio*. Read the poem to the children. Talk about what is happening to the porwigles (tadpoles) and discuss the life cycle of frogs, providing pictures if the children are unfamiliar with the process.
- Ask the children if porwigles, or tadpoles, could pretend to be whales. Talk about the difference and point out that the poet is deliberately using an extreme contrast in size to make the poem funny.
- Now ask the children if they have ever heard a similar poem or rhyme in which, one by one, things disappear. Link the poem to 'Ten Green Bottles' or 'Five Little Ducks', explaining that it is a traditional rhyme that the author has rewritten, using porwigles.
- Look at the rhyming words in the poem, particularly words that rhyme with numbers (*dive/five; explore/four* and so on). Discuss other poems that use number rhymes, reading out the rhyming lines, such as *One, two, three, four, five, once I caught a fish alive.*
- Read the poem again, using an enlarged version, and mask words such as *Pretending.* Ask the children to use the context and meaning to work out what the word might be, then provide clues, such as the first few letters.
- Ask the children to help you to find all the words that share the common letter pattern *ing*, for example *wriggling, trying.* Split the words into segments (*try-ing*) and show the children that recognising parts of words can help us read the whole word.
- Now read the poem again, modelling reading with tone and expression. Ask the children to join in with different sections. For example, the whole class could read the first four lines of each verse as well as the last two lines (which are almost identical). One or two children could read the fifth and sixth line of each verse plus the endings of the penultimate and final verse.

Activities

- Provide copies of the poem for the children to highlight all the words ending in *ing*. Display lists of verbs, showing what happens when *ing* is added to a root word.
- With adult support, let the children write substitute verses, using alternative words. For example, brainstorm substitutes for the verb *wriggling*, such as *swimming, nestling.* Replace nouns – you could have *Went to find the pond* instead of *Went to find the sea*, for example. Provide writing frames, if necessary.

Extension/further reading

Encourage more able children to change some of the words in traditional rhymes such as 'Twinkle, twinkle little star'.

Make collections of other alternative nursery rhymes and traditional poems (with the original printed on one side of a page and the alternative version on the other) and use them in guided reading sessions.

Link the poem to science work on life cycles and, if possible, give the children the opportunity to observe tadpoles. Follow this up by drawing the development from tadpole to frog, in a cyclical design.

Twinkle Twinkle Chocolate Bar compiled by John Foster (OUP) is an anthology of rhymes for the very young. Children could learn Lewis Carroll's rhyme: *Twinkle, twinkle, little bat! How I wonder what you're at! Up above the world you fly, Like a tea-tray in the sky.* 'Monday's Child is Red and Spotty' by Colin McNaughton can be found in *The Orchard Book of Funny Poems* compiled by Wendy Cope (Orchard Books).

1: 3: T1: to reinforce and apply their word-level skills through shared and guided reading

1: 3: T2: to use phonological, contextual, grammatical and graphic knowledge to work out, predict and check the meanings of unfamiliar words and to make sense of what they read

1: 3: W6: to investigate and learn spellings of verbs with 'ing' (present tense) endings

words ending in 'ing'

each verse begins with a number

number decreases at beginning of each verse (similar to 'Ten Green Bottles' and 'Five Little Ducks')

Porwigles

Six porwigles
Wriggling in a pool,
Pretending to be whales
And trying to keep cool.
One porwigle whale
Tried a flying dive—
When they had a tail count
There were only five.

Five porwigles
Wriggling in a pool,
Pretending to be whales
And trying to keep cool.
One porwigle whale
Went off to explore—
When they had a tail count
There were only four.

Four porwigles
Wriggling in a pool,
Pretending to be whales
And trying to keep cool.
One porwigle whale
Went to find the sea—
When they had a tail count
There were only three.

Three porwigles
Wriggling in a pool,
Pretending to be whales
And trying to keep cool.
One porwigle whale
Didn't like the view—
When they had a tail count
There were only two.

Two porwigles
Wriggling in a pool,
Pretending to be whales
And trying to keep cool.
One porwigle whale
Went to see his Mum—
Left the last one on his own,
There is only one.

One porwigle
Wriggling in a pool,
Feeling rather lonely
And trying to keep cool.
One all alone porwigle
Jumped onto a log—
And you couldn't count *his* tail
Because he's turned into a frog!

Julie Holder

(Porwigle is an old English name for a tadpole.)

repeated lines

this line changes in each verse

italic text and exclamation mark for expression when reading

shows what has happened to tadpole (life cycle of a frog)

names can change over time

rhyming words

1: 3: T11: to collect class and individual favourite poems for class anthologies, participate in reading aloud

1: 3: S3: to read familiar texts aloud with pace and expression appropriate to the grammar, e.g. pausing at full stops, raising voice for questions

1: 3: W5: to recognise words by common spelling patterns

Here is the Nose by Clyde Watson

P 148

Background

This is a poem which echoes other familiar rhymes, for example:

Here are the lady's knives and forks,
Here is the lady's table,
Here is the lady's looking class,
And here is the baby's cradle.

The rhythm and repetition of the words *Here are* and *Here is* are the same as in Clyde Watson's version. In addition, 'Here is the Nose' bears some similarity to the nursery rhyme 'The house that Jack built' in that it echoes the rhythm, although it is not cumulative in the same way.

So Clyde Watson's poem uses a familiar structure, repetition and rhythm but instead tells of a greedy boy who eats a blueberry pie, humorously recounting what happens to him. It links with other poems that provide alternatives to traditional rhymes (see pages 84 and 88).

Shared reading and discussing the text

- Read the poem to the children. Talk about what happens to the boy and why he ran for the door (to escape punishment for being greedy).
- Ask the children if this text reminds them of any other poems. Read the example above and any others such as the rhyme beginning *Here is the church and here is the steeple...*
- Now read the poem again, with the children joining in with plenty of expression. You could add actions, although ensure that 'smacks' are just taps!
- Look carefully at the structure of the poem and highlight how each verse uses a different part of the body. Look at how other parts of the body could have been used, for example *Here are the Hands* instead of *Here are the Arms*, or *Here are the Legs* instead of *Here are the Feet.*
- Now take the first line from one of the verses and point out that the words are always in the same order. Experiment with different word orders (you could use the words printed individually on cards). For example, change *Here are the Eyes that looked high and low* to *The eyes that looked high and low are here.* Compare the different effects and explain that poets think carefully about the order of the words they use.
- Talk about each verse of the poem and the pattern of rhyme (rhyming couplets). Discuss how this makes it fun to read.

Activities

- Work with a guided group to look at rhyme. Highlight the rhyming couplets and talk about whether the words always share the same spelling, for example *high* and *pie.* Make lists of rhyming words.
- Provide the children with a writing frame to write their own versions of the poem. They could substitute *blueberry pie* for *chocolate cake*, and so on. Supply class lists of rhyming words to help them.
- Cut out words from the poem to allow the children to investigate changing the word order to make alternative sentences.
- Use the poem to encourage more able children to write other poems with repetitive patterns with a given first line, for example *Here is the girl with the clean white dress...*
- Play oral rhyming games with less able children, such as 'Rhyming tennis' in which they pick up a card with a word on it and have to think of a word that rhymes.

Extension/further reading

Make links to work in science on the different parts of the body.

In PSHE and citizenship, use the theme of the poem – greed – to talk about being selfish. Discuss other poems or stories that illustrate the importance of sharing with others, such as *The Selfish Giant* by Oscar Wilde (Puffin).

The poems beginning *Here is the ostrich straight and tall* and *Here is the sea, the wavy sea* can be found in *This Little Puffin...* compiled by Elizabeth Matterson (Puffin).

1: 3: T10: to compare and contrast preferences and common themes in stories and poems

Here is the Nose

Here is the Nose that smelled something sweet
And led the search for a bite to eat.

Here are the Feet that followed the Nose
Around the kitchen on ten Tiptoes.

Here are the Eyes that looked high and low
Till they spotted six pans sitting all in a row.

Here are the Arms that reached up high
To bring down a fresh-baked blueberry pie.

Here is the Mouth that opened up wide.
Here are the Hands that put pie inside.

Here is the Tongue that licked the tin
And lapped up the juice running down the Chin.

Here is the Stomach that growled for more.
Here are the Legs that ran for the door.

Here are the Ears that heard a whack.
Here is the Bottom that felt a smack!

Clyde Watson

predictable pattern

repeated beginning of 1st line in each verse

different part of the body in each verse

same word order each time

humour

rhymes with same sound but different spelling

rhymes with same spelling

1: 3: T16: to compose own poetic sentences, using repetitive patterns, carefully selected sentences and imagery

1: 3: S4: to learn about word order, e.g. by re-ordering sentences, predicting words from previous text, grouping a range of words that might 'fit', and discussing the reasons why

There Was an Old Woman by Charles Causley

P 149

Background

This poem continues the theme of alternative versions of traditional rhymes. Here the rhyme beginning *There was an old woman who lived in a shoe...* is changed to make an amusing version of an old woman who becomes a prisoner after attacking a policeman. It has a strong rhythm and rhyme that make it ideal for reading aloud, although some of the vocabulary will be unfamiliar to Year 1 children and will need explaining. The poem can be used as a model for writing other alternative versions. The following two anonymous versions could also be referred to:

There was an old woman called Nothing-at-all,
Who lived in a dwelling exceedingly small;
A man stretched his mouth to its utmost
extent,
And down at one gulp house and old
woman went.

There was an old woman lived under a hill,
And if she's not gone, she lives there still,
Baked apples she sold, and cranberry pies,
And she's the old woman that never told
lies.

Shared reading and discussing the text

- Read the poem to the children with expression. Discuss carefully what happens to the old woman and why. Look at the unfamiliar vocabulary such as *tattered* and *spectacles* as well as expressions such as *I don't give a fig...* and ensure that the meaning of each line is clear.
- Ask the children if this reminds them of any other poems. Read the examples above as well as the traditional version and compare what happens to the old woman and the different effects. Make links to other alternative versions of traditional rhymes, for example 'Porwigles' (see page 84) and 'Here is the Nose' (see page 86), explaining that this is another poem for the class collection.
- Now read it again, with the children joining in with plenty of expression. Different groups of children could read the old woman's words and others the judge's, with the class joining in with the last line. You could also choose different children to act out the role of the old woman, the policeman and the judge.
- Look at the long vowel sound in the word *hoot* and brainstorm with the children other words that share this sound, for example *boot, loot, scoot*. In addition look at words that share the sound but not spelling pattern, for example *suit, fruit*, and make lists of words that share the same pattern.

Activities

- Work with a guided group to look at rhyme and highlight the pattern of rhyming couplets (apart from the last verse, which has an extra line added, making the first and third lines rhyme). Talk about the rhyming words and whether they always share the same spelling, for example *said* and *bread*. Compile lists of rhyming words.
- Let the children go on to use the lists of rhyming words to write rhyming couplets with a given sentence starter, for example *There was an old woman who lived in a box* (to which the children could add *Who got terribly frightened when she saw a fox*).
- Provide the children with copies of the poem for them to highlight all the unfamiliar words. With a partner they can then try to find other words with the same meaning, for example *beat – patch*. Encourage them to first guess the meaning by reading the whole sentence.

Extension/further reading

Look at examples of stories and poems in which children did not follow rules and discuss what happened to them, such as 'Adventures of Isabel' by Ogden Nash in *The Orchard Book of Funny Poems* (Orchard Books). 'There Was an Old Man' by James Kirkup is in *A First Poetry Book* compiled by John Foster (OUP).

1: 3: T10: to compare and contrast preferences and common themes in stories and poems

There Was an Old Woman

There was an old woman of Chester-le-Street
Who chased a policeman all over his beat.

She shattered his helmet and tattered his clothes
And knocked his new spectacles clean off his nose.

"I'm afraid," said the Judge, "I must make it quite clear
You can't get away with that sort of thing here."

"I can and I will," the old woman she said,
"And I don't give a fig for your water and bread.

"I don't give a hoot for your cold prison cell,
And your bolts and your bars and your handcuffs as well.

"I've never been one to do just as I'm bid.
You can put me in jail for a year!"
So they did.

Charles Causley

familiar opening but then a contrast with original version

unfamiliar words

a saying meaning 'I don't care'

long vowel phoneme 'oo'

rhyming couplet

the name of a place

words that rhyme but have different spellings

same sound and spelling

1st and 3rd line rhyme

additional line for emphasis

1: 3: T16: to compose own poetic sentences, using repetitive patterns, carefully selected sentences and imagery

1: 3: W1: the common spelling patterns for the long vowel phoneme *oo* (long as in *moon*):
- to identify phonemes in speech and writing
- to blend phonemes for reading
- to segment words into phonemes for spelling

When the Wind Blows by John Foster

P 150

Background

'When the Wind Blows' is a contemporary poem with a patterned structure. It echoes the second line of the nursery rhyme 'Hush-a-bye baby': *When the wind blows the cradle will rock* (which rhymes with the first line *Hush-a-bye baby on the tree-top*). The opening line of 'When the Wind Blows' is a good example of the use of a repeated line – it appears at the beginning of each verse – and the poem provides an excellent model for a similar poem to be written. Links can be made with other poems on wind and weather such as 'The March Wind' (see page 92) and 'The Sound of the Wind' (see page 94).

Shared reading and discussing the text

- Read the poem, then talk about what the wind is doing. Now read it again, with the children joining in, and choose some children to make sound effects with their voices for some of the verbs. Talk about the effect of the wind blowing and the sounds it causes the coats, scarves, branches and other things in the poem to make. If it is a windy day, take the children outside to observe what happens in the wind – can they see leaves swirling, for example?
- Ask the children to spot something that is the same in each verse (the first line). Talk about why the poet has done this; what effect it has. Look at the contrast between the first and second line and discuss the structure of the second line (noun, verb, noun, verb). Talk about why this is more effective than saying *The coats were flapping and the scarves were fluttering.* Explain that it helps to emphasise the movement of the wind.
- Discuss the particular verbs used to describe the movement, for example *Coats flap.* Talk about whether branches really groan and leaves really mutter and why the poet has chosen these words. Ensure that the children are familiar with all the terms. Highlight the verbs in the poem and then create a new poem from the verbs (for example, *Washing flaps, litter flutters...*).
- Talk about the contrast between the rhythm of lines 1 and 2 in each verse (apart from the last verse). Ask the children to clap the rhythm of each verse (four syllables in the first line, and five, six or seven in the second line). Discuss the final verse of the poem and how it changes from a couplet to three lines, as it contrasts the calm inside to the wild weather outside.
- Look at the rhyming words, such as *flutter* and *mutter,* and using magnetic letters show how the words share the same letter patterns. Identify which letters change each time. Build up a list of words that share the same rhyming and spelling patterns, for example *flutter, mutter, butter, shutter, gutter...*

Activities

- Model writing an alternative poem, replacing the line *When the wind blows* with *When the sun shines* or *When the storm comes.* Brainstorm all the common features of sunny or rainy days, then create a new version. For example, *When the storm comes, Clouds blacken, lightning flashes. When the storm comes, Wind howls, thunder crashes...*
- Provide the children with a writing frame, with the opening line repeated as you have just modelled, and ask them to write their own weather poem.
- The use of onomatopoeia with words such as *swish* and *clatter* helps to create the effect of sound as well as movement. Use these words to begin a collection of words that create particular effects. These can be used for further poetry writing.

Extension/further reading

Further poems about the wind include 'Wind Song' by Lillian Moore and 'Dark Windy Night' by Anne English in *A Very First Poetry Book* compiled by John Foster (OUP), 'The Wind' in *A Child's Garden of Verses* by Robert Louis Stevenson (Dorling Kindersley) and 'The North Wind Doth Blow' (Anon) in *Once Upon a Rhyme: 101 Poems for Young Children* edited by Sara and Stephen Corrin (Puffin).

1: 3: T9: to read a variety of poems on similar themes, e.g. families, school, food

1: 3: T15: to use poems or parts of poems as models for own writing, e.g. by substituting words or elaborating on the text

1: 3: T16: to compose own poetic sentences, using repetitive patterns, carefully selected sentences and imagery

When the Wind Blows

When the wind blows
Coats flap, scarves flutter.

When the wind blows
Branches groan, leaves mutter.

When the wind blows
Curtains swish, papers scatter.

When the wind blows
Gates creak, dustbins clatter.

When the wind blows
Doors slam, windows rattle.

When the wind blows
Inside is a haven,
Outside is a battle.

John Foster

high-frequency word

(box) = verb; 1st 5 verses are structured around verbs; they almost work on their own

repeated phrase gives patterned structure

sound effects (onomatopoeia)

short phrasing (noun, verb, noun, verb) creates sense of the activity of the wind

change in pattern – additional line for ending

rhyming words share spelling pattern

a place of peace

contrast in meaning

a struggle

1: 3: S3: to read familiar texts aloud with pace and expression appropriate to the grammar, e.g. pausing at full stops, raising voice for questions

1: 3: W5: to recognise words by common spelling patterns

1: 3: W8: to gather new words from reading and shared experiences, and to make collections of personal interest or significant words and words linked to particular topics

The March Wind

P 151

Background

This poem continues the theme of the wind, this time in a strong, lively rhythm. The poet personifies the wind, using *I* and uses an assortment of strong verbs to describe the action of the wind. It could form part of a class collection on the theme of wind or weather, and in particular lends itself to reciting aloud, with children enacting the movement of the wind.

Shared reading and discussing the text

- Read the poem to the children with expression, then read it again slowly using an enlarged copy and a pointer, so all the class can join in. Read it a third time, with the children creating sound effects, particularly for *Woo-oo-oo-ooo!*
- Ask the children who *I* is in the poem. Give examples of what *I* does to help the children to see it is the wind personified. Now look carefully at all the things the wind does and discuss whether the children have witnessed these themselves when they have been out on windy days.
- Discuss the time of year the poem represents and highlight clues, such as *leaves in flocks of brown* and *frozen earth*, and perhaps whether this changes in the final verse with *wake the flowers from sleep.*
- Look carefully at the rhythm of the poem, asking the children to tap the rhythm with you as you read it.
- Look also at the rhyme of the poem on alternate lines and highlight the rhyming words.
- Examine the words containing long vowel sounds, particularly *ee*, as in *sweep* and *sleep*, and compile a list of words with the same sound, for example *deep.*
- Look closely with the children at all the actions of the wind and discuss what type of words these are – verbs.

Activities

- Ask the children to compile a list of verbs from the poem describing the wind's movements (*whistle, toss, shake, whirl, send, strew, sweep, blow, wake*) and brainstorm others.
- Using the list of verbs, more able children can go on to make their own poetic sentences, pretending they are the wind, for example:

> I heap the leaves in great huge piles,
> That's what I like to do.
> I scatter the rubbish on for miles,
> And leave it there for you.

Provide less able children with sentences to which they can add appropriate verbs.

- Taking sentences from the poem to show the different actions of the wind, for example *I toss the branches up and down*, children can rewrite and illustrate them.
- Provide the children with words from the poem containing the *ee* phoneme (*sweep, sleep*) and ask them to use magnetic letters to make new words, for example *creep, deep...* Allow them to create nonsense words, if they wish, such as *fleep* and *tweep.*

Extension/further reading

Read a range of poems about the wind with the children in guided reading sessions and collect examples for a class collection on the theme of weather, for example 'The Wind' by James Reeves in *A First Poetry Book* compiled by John Foster (OUP) and 'The Wind' by Dorothy Gradon in *Once Upon a Rhyme: 101 Poems for Young Children* edited by Sara and Stephen Corrin (Puffin).

Link the activities to work in art and geography, the children making drawings and paintings of windy days and the effects of different weather. Form these into a classroom display, adding children's descriptions or poems of windy, snowy, sunny and rainy days.

1: 3: T9: to read a variety of poems on similar themes, e.g. families, school, food

1: 3: T11: to collect class and individual favourite poems for class anthologies, participate in reading aloud

THE MARCH WIND

I come to work as well as play;
I'll tell you what I do;
I whistle all the livelong day,
"Woo-oo-oo-oo! Woo-oo!"
I toss the branches up and down R
And shake them to and fro,
I whirl the leaves in flocks of brown, R
And send them high and low.
I strew the twigs upon the ground,
The frozen earth I sweep;
I blow the children round and round
And wake the flowers from sleep.

Anonymous

title indicates time of year

use of 'I' to personify the wind

repetitive pattern – 'I' followed by a strong verb

change in pattern to emphasise sound of the wind

alternate lines rhyme

clues given to time of year/season

long vowel sound 'ee'

season about to change from winter to spring – are flowers really asleep?

1: 3: T16: to compose own poetic sentences, using repetitive patterns, carefully selected sentences and imagery

1: 3: W1: the common spelling patterns for the long vowel phoneme *ee*:
- to identify phonemes in speech and writing
- to blend phonemes for reading
- to segment words into phonemes for spelling

The Sound of the Wind

by Christina Rossetti

P 152

Background

This well-known poem by Christina Rossetti continues the theme of the wind. Whereas 'When the Wind Blows' (see page 90) presents a vivid picture of the movement of the wind, and 'The March Wind' personifies the wind (see page 92), this poem describes the sound of the wind and its destructive effects. The rhythm and rhyme in the poem makes it an excellent choice for reading aloud with expression.

Shared reading and discussing the text

- Read the poem to the children with expression and ask them to close their eyes and tell you what they saw and imagined as they listened. Ask the children whether this poem is similar to any others they have read.
- Now look carefully at the first verse. Discuss why the poet uses *rainy sound* and talk about what the children think is a rainy sound. Look at the use of the verb *moaning* and encourage the children to tell you why it has been used – does the wind really moan? And why does the sea have a *windy sound*? Relate this to any experiences the children have had of the sea when it is windy.
- Focusing on the second verse, ask the children what happens to trees and gardens sometimes when it is very windy. Have they ever seen fruit that has been blown off the trees onto the ground? In the penultimate line the poet mentions the ships again (*Oh will the ships go down, go down*). Help the children to see that this builds up tension and makes the reader aware of the poet's concern. Relate this to shipwrecks and disasters at sea, which were more common in the past.
- After discussing the meaning of the words and effects in the poem, read it again with the children. Do this several times and create expression with different levels of volume. You could also add sound effects for moans and rainy sounds, as well as for apples tumbling from the tree.
- Examine the rhyming pattern of the poem (the alternate lines ending in *sound; town, down; tree, sea*) and talk about how this helps make it pleasurable to read aloud. Ask the children to point out all the words that rhyme and talk about the pattern changes in the second verse which also help to add to the tension and sense of danger.
- Point to the question marks and ask the children what these are. Now underline the questions in the first and second verse. Say the sentences together and talk about the way the voice changes when it is a question – that is, it goes up at the end.

Activities

- Give groups of children copies of the poem to practise reading aloud with expression. They could either read the poem to the class in a plenary session, or they could record their versions onto audio tape.
- Ask the children to generate rhyming strings from *town*; they can do this with magnetic letters. Ensure that they know it is the onset that they need to change.
- In guided writing, look at the question from the last verse of the poem. Now model an alternative question, for example *Oh will the trees fall down, fall down on a windy night?* Ask the children to think of alternative questions to fit those two lines of the poem.
- Ask more able children to write an alternative poem. Provide a writing frame with an opening line such as *The wind has such a stormy sound.* Less able children can be given the poem with some of the rhyming words missing for them to fill in alternatives.

Extension/further reading

In PSHE and citizenship discuss the dangers of water and how to keep safe, making sure the children know to stay close to an adult.

Read together 'The Storm' by Sara Coleridge in *Time for a Rhyme* chosen by Fiona Waters (Orion Children's Books) and 'There are Big Waves' by Eleanor Farjeon in *Once Upon a Rhyme: 101 Poems for Young Children* edited by Sara and Stephen Corrin (Puffin).

1: 3: T9: to read a variety of poems on similar themes, e.g. families, school, food

1: 3: T11: to collect class and individual favourite poems for class anthologies, participate in reading aloud

THE SOUND OF THE WIND

The wind has such a rainy sound
Moaning through the town,
The sea has such a windy sound –
Will the ships go down?

The apples in the orchard
Tumble from their tree –
Oh will the ships go down, go down,
In the windy sea?

Christina Rossetti

poem is focusing on the wind's sounds

repetitive pattern

does the wind really moan?

sink

verb chosen to create 'sound'

question repeated from 1st verse but elaborated

on windy days the wind affects the sea, and ships can be put in danger

how can sounds be rainy?

why does the sea have a windy sound?

fruit trees planted together

repeated phrase for dramatic effect

question mark signals that voice should go up slightly at end of sentence

1: 3: T16: to compose own poetic sentences, using repetitive patterns, carefully selected sentences and imagery

1: 3: S7: to add question marks to questions

When I'm Big by Debi Gliori

P 153

Background

This extract is from a story about a little girl who dreams of being grown up. It is triggered by the child being told it is past her bedtime and, with indignation, she goes on to describe all the things she wants to do when she is big. After this extract, the child reverses the role of parent and child and puts Mum and Dad to bed. The story ends with a nice twist, as when the girl finds herself alone downstairs at night, she wants to be little again, so she can squeeze in between Mum and Dad in bed in *the safest place in the world.* This extract is written with a strong repeating pattern and can be used as a good model for writing.

Shared reading and discussing the text

- Introduce the text by looking at the title together. Ask the children if they have ever wished they were big and could stay up late and do as they like.
- Read the extract, then encourage the children to talk about the different things they think they would like to do when they are big. Now re-read the text, with the children joining in. Model using a range of reading strategies to read unfamiliar words such as *gumboots* and *triffids.* Ensure that the children understand the meanings.
- Look at the different things the child in the extract would like to do in the future compared with what she does now, for example swimming with whales in the sea as opposed to having a bath. Compile a list with the children.
- How would the children feel in a situation in which the roles of parents and children were reversed? Ask them to work in pairs, using their imagination to decide on something they would like to do if they were the parents in their homes, for example they might want to make their 'children' eat all their dinner, go to bed at eight o'clock, and so on.
- Talk about the ending of the story (see above) and discuss why it may not always be best to be 'big', for example you miss out on all the helpful things parents and carers can do for you.

Activities

- Ask the children to rehearse orally sentences beginning *When I'm big...*, such as *When I'm big I'm going to climb the highest mountain in the world on my own.* They can then write three sentences focusing on something they want to do, something they want to wear and something they want to eat. The sentences could be combined to form a class story. Emphasise that they should try to think of things that are very unlikely – playing with tigers, for example. This made the original funny and they need to do the same.
- Provide some examples of sentences from the text for the children to use awareness of grammar and context to decipher unfamiliar words, for example *I'm going to drive the trolley round the shops with Dad in it instead of the other way round.* They can then read their sentences in a plenary session.

Extension/further reading

If you have a copy of the book and children are familiar with the whole story, ask them to retell the story onto tape using traditional story language, for example *There was once a little girl who dreamed of being big...*

Ask the children to rehearse role-playing the story, working together in groups to pool ideas and ensuring that they show what happens in the beginning (something that their parents/ carers are asking them to do that they feel is unfair), the middle (saying what their wish list would be for what they want to do when they are grown up) and the end (being contented to be young). They could perform this for the class. They could then go on to write down their own versions of the story.

Link the text to work in history about growing up and the different generations of a family.

Books which explore the theme of growing up include *You'll Soon Grow Into Them, Titch* by Pat Hutchins (Red Fox). *Oh, Little Jack* by Inga Moore (Walker Books) tells the story of a little rabbit who comes to realise that being small has its advantages.

1: 3: T6: to prepare and retell stories orally, identifying and using some of the more formal features of story language

When I'm Big

When I'm big, I'm going to stay up as late as I like and make myself marshmallows on toast instead of going to bed.

When I'm big, I'm going swimming with the whales in the deep blue sea instead of puddling about in the bath.

When I'm big, I'm going to wear a bird-suit and gumboots all day long instead of a jumper and dungarees.

When I'm big, I'm going to have a huge back garden with sand mountains that touch the sky and a lake in the middle instead of a sandpit and a paddling pool.

When I'm big, I'm going to drive the trolley round the shops with Dad in it instead of the other way round.

When I'm big, I'm going to grow triffids and Venus fly-traps and man-eating orchids instead of mustard and cress.

Annotations:

- *contrast*
- *repetition of phrase*
- *each statement presents a different wish*
- *opposite actions show contrast and child's contrary nature*
- *wellingtons*
- *contrast*
- *each sentence shows greater daring and independence, showing frustration of child who cannot stay up late*
- *contrast*
- *role reversal*
- *human-eating plants from science fiction*
- *insect-eating plants*
- *exotic flowers*

1: 3: T14: to write stories using simple settings, e.g. based on previous reading

1: 3: S2: to use awareness of the grammar of a sentence to decipher new or unfamiliar words, e.g. predict text from the grammar, read on, leave a gap and re-read

But Martin!

by June Counsel

P 154

Background

But Martin! tells the story of four very different children who are making their way to school when they meet a Martian. They all become great friends and the story and humour revolves around how Martin reacts to events. This extract describes the differences between Martin and the children, both in appearance and behaviour. Although the story is set in a realistic setting, the inclusion of a Martian as a character brings a strong element of fantasy. So further work on stories from fantasy worlds could be carried out in addition to the focus on patterned and predictable structures. The extract also provides plenty of opportunities for discussion of different characters.

Shared reading and discussing the text

- Read the extract, then talk about how the characters felt at the beginning of the story until they met Martin. Encourage the children to discuss how they felt when they first started the new school year.
- Discuss with the children the different characters and how soon they realised that one character was not what they might expect. Draw up a chart comparing the characters, with *Names* and *Appearance* as headings, and highlight the differences between them. Focus on Martin's characteristics in particular.
- Read the story again, asking the children to join in with the refrain *but Martin...*; pause for emphasis before saying what Martin did each time. Talk about the use of patterned language, for example *Lee skipped, Billy chased, Lloyd jumped and Angela cartwheeled, but Martin... floated!* Show how this emphasises the contrast between Martin and the other characters.
- Look closely with the children at the use of capitalisation in the extract. Ask them when we use capital letters and show them that in this story, not only do they show a new sentence, and are used for people's names, but they are used to make words stand out. Discuss how this highlights the difference between Martin and the other characters in the story.
- Explain that this story happened in the past and some words show this, for example those with *ed* endings. Use acetate over the text, or highlight words on an enlarged photocopy, and ask the children to point out all the words ending in *ed.* Ensure they understand the difference between present and past by discussing events happening now and those that happened before. Explain that *ed* is the most common ending of words to show that something happened in the past.

Activities

- Using the chart from shared text work, model writing a sentence to describe Martin, with headings of what he looked like. The children can then complete their own versions.
- Brainstorm with the children a possible ending to the story. Write this during a shared writing session, emphasising the predictable structure. Ask the children to go on to complete their own versions, but first ensure that they have all been given the opportunity to rehearse sentences orally before they write them. Provide less able children with key words to help them form sentences and, if possible, provide additional adult help to ensure that they have the confidence to make a start. They could be given sentence starters to help them complete the story, interspersed with the repeated refrain *but Martin.* The book ends with Martin going home in his flying saucer. Compare this with the children's own ideas for an ending.
- Ask more able children to write a further episode of what happens on another day when Martin goes to school.

Extension/further reading

Brainstorm with the children what would happen if a strange alien came to their school. In shared writing, compose a class story.

Celebrate diversity by compiling charts of different eye and hair colours in the class.

The children may enjoy *Funnybones* by Janet and Allan Ahlberg (Puffin), which features skeletons as fantasy characters.

1: 3: T10: to compare and contrast preferences and common themes in stories

1: 3: T13: to write about significant incidents from known stories

But Martin!

That first morning back at school
Lee's lips turned down
Lloyd's head hung down
Billy's brows drew down
And Angela's tears fell down
but that was before they found
MARTIN!

Lee's face was smooth and golden
Lloyd's face was round and brown
Billy's face was square and red
And Angela's face was long and white
but Martin's face was
GREEN!

Lee's hair was black and silky
Lloyd's hair was black and bouncy
Billy's hair was red and spiky
And Angela's hair was fair and floaty
but Martin's hair
WASN'T THERE!
(he just had these)

When they saw him
Lee giggled
Lloyd shouted

Billy whistled
and Angela gasped
but Martin
BLEEPED!

Then they began to play.
Lee skipped
Billy chased
Lloyd jumped
and Angela cartwheeled
but Martin
FLOATED!

The bell rang and
Lee stood still
Lloyd stopped dead
Billy wobbled
and Angela froze
but Martin
VANISHED!

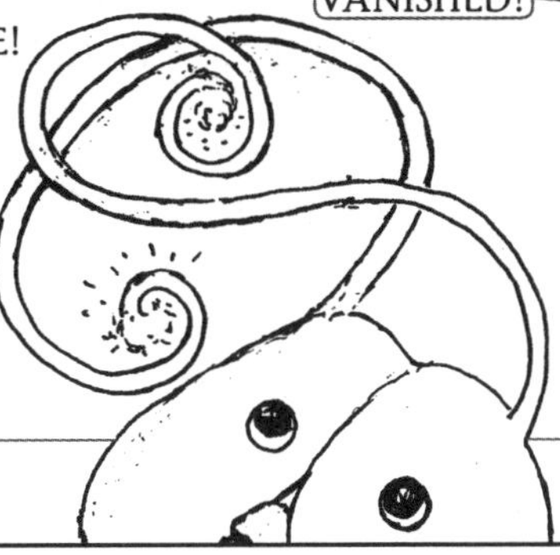

familiar setting

capitalisation for start of sentence

capitalisation for name

focus on faces

contrasting features shown in physical description

focus on hair

fantasy character

focus on actions

'ed' endings for past tense

repetition of structure – Martin is always different from the other children

capitalisation for emphasis

1: 3: W6: to investigate and learn spellings of verbs with 'ed' (past tense) endings)

1: 3: S5: to investigate other common uses of capitalisation, e.g. for personal titles (*Mr, Miss*), headings, book titles, emphasis

A first night away

P 155

Background

This is a non-fiction recount of a child's experience of staying away from home for the first time. It will provide a familiar context and many children will identify with the feeling of being unhappy at being separated from their parents and carers. It can be linked to 'How my body has changed' (see page 102) and 'I came to Britain from Jamaica' (see page 104). The text provides a good model for children to write their own recount of a visit, for example staying with a friend. It can also reinforce the concept of sequencing.

Shared reading and discussing the text

- Introduce the subject of visiting friends and ask the children if they have slept at a friend's house. Talk about how they felt – excited, worried, and so on. Now read the text to the children and when you have finished discuss how Sam felt.
- Explain that this is a recount that tells what happened in order. Now read an enlarged copy of the text, with the children joining in; then deconstruct the recount with them, using a planning sheet labelled *First... Next... Then... Later... Finally...* and note the sequence of events – for example, *First, Sam packed his things; second, his mum drove him to his friend's house...*
- Talk to the children about important words that give us clues about the order in which things happen, such as *first, when, then, next, later.* Now ask the children to help you highlight these words in the text. Establish that the text has a clear beginning, middle and end.
- Ask the children if this event is happening to Sam now or if it happened in the past. Explain that when we write about things in a recount we write about the past and some of the words change to show this, for example *pack* becomes *packed* and *watch* becomes *watched.* Write the words and ask the children what has been added to each word to show it happened in the past. Explain that we often add *ed* to a word to show it is in the past.

Activities

- Model putting events into a sequence. Put different events from the recount onto card. Then ask several children to hold up different sentences and ask them to line up in the right order. Highlight the clue words, such as *first, then, next, finally,* to help the children order themselves correctly.
- Give pairs of children a series of statements from the recount to put into the correct sequence. Encourage them to work together to assess whether the order on which they have decided is correct.
- Ask a group to track *ed* words in the text to share with the class in a plenary session.

Extension/further reading

Continue with a series of writing tasks based around *A first...*, for example a first day at school, a first trip on a boat/plane/train, a first visit to the seaside. Provide writing frames for children's own individual recounts, and in guided group work help the children to rehearse their sequences orally before writing. If the recount is based on a common school experience, a writing frame that the children complete at a computer may encourage pairs of children to work together to produce their recount, perhaps with a less able child helping with recalling events.

Make links with PSHE and citizenship work on emotions and in particular feeling scared. Use this as a focus in circle time, with the children being given a sentence starter such as *I feel scared when...*

Read poems and stories that link with the idea of feeling scared or being away from home, such as 'In the Dark' by Jane Pridmore from *A First Poetry Book* compiled by John Foster (OUP) or 'The Bogus-Boo' by James Reeves from *Poems for 7-year-olds and under* chosen by Helen Nicoll (Puffin). Other first events are explored in *Edward's First Swimming Party* by Rosemary Wells (Walker Books) and *My First Day at School* by Rebecca Hunter in the *First Times* series (Evans Brothers Ltd).

1: 3: T18: to read recounts and begin to recognise generic structure, e.g. ordered sequence of events, use of words like *first, next, after, when*

1: 3: T20: to write simple recounts linked to topics of interest/study or to personal experience, using the language of texts read as models for own writing

A first night away

introductory sentences help reader to find out 'who', 'when' and 'where'

Going to stay away from home for the first time can be very exciting. This is what happened when Sam, a five-year-old boy, went to stay with his best friend, Tom.

'ed' endings used in past tense

sequencing words

beginning

3 steps in sequence

First, Sam packed his pyjamas and clean clothes in a bag. Next, he packed a few toys, not forgetting his teddy. Then it was time to go. Sam's mum drove him to Tom's house, and Sam went to play with Tom in his bedroom.

middle

Sam spent a good day with his friend. In the afternoon they had a trip to the park. They each had an ice cream. When they went back to Tom's house there was time to play with Tom's toys and watch TV. Then they ate their tea together. After that, they had fun in the bath together.

end

'ed' endings used in past tense

Later at bedtime, Sam began to miss home. Tom's mum read them a bedtime story and gave them both a goodnight kiss. But Sam couldn't get to sleep and finally went downstairs. He felt very sad, so his mum had to come and fetch him. He was wrapped up in a blanket and taken home to his own bed. Sam was disappointed that he did not stay the night at his friend's house, but perhaps he will when he is bigger.

1: 3: W6: to investigate and learn spellings of verbs with 'ed' (past tense) endings

How my body has changed

P 156

Background

This is a non-fiction account of a child's physical development from a baby to school age. The text provides a good example of a recount, and young children will easily be able to identify with it. The use of captions to accompany the pictures makes it accessible, and children can use the text as a model for producing a recount of their own development. It can be linked to previous work on features of recounts, 'A first night away' (see page 100).

Shared reading and discussing the text

- Look at an enlarged version of the text with the children and ask them to look closely at the pictures to guess what it is all about. Read the title and explain that this recount is about how one child has grown.
- Now read the text, using a pointer, with the children joining in. Pause after each sentence to look again at the pictures. Explain that pictures in non-fiction books give us information, just as the writing does.
- Discuss the children's memories of learning to ride a tricycle, and other events that showed they were growing and changing. Ask them if they remember learning to crawl, or to walk, and explain that it is very difficult to remember things from when they were very small, but looking at photographs and talking to parents and carers can help.
- Encourage the children to talk about what they remember about recounts and ask them to tell you the clue words that are useful for showing us the correct order of events (*first, next, later, finally* and so on). Now ask the children to help you find these words in the text and highlight them. Talk about the order and how this relates to the child growing up.
- Explain to the children that they will be writing recounts of their own and that it helps, when they are writing, if they learn to spell words that they use often. Choose one or two words from the text that are in high-frequency word list 1, such as *could*, and talk about the fact that there are some words that we just need to learn as they are not written as they sound. Ask the children which part of the word *could* is difficult (*oul*) and explain that sometimes a little saying can help us remember the letters. Tell them that for the *o-u-l-d*, we can say, *oh you lucky duck*. Make a poster displaying this for the classroom.

Activities

- Work with a group of children to transfer the details of the text onto a chart showing the typical growth of a baby and toddler – at a few days old... a few months old... and so on.
- Provide a writing frame for children to produce their own accounts of their early development. Ensure that you model an example first. Use these to form children's own books, or a class book including photographs where possible.
- Provide less able children with paper divided into boxes (the number of boxes will depend on their ability) and ask them to draw something they could do when they were a baby, as a toddler and now. Ask them to write a caption underneath each picture.
- Provide copies of the text with the captions blanked off, for more able children to write their own.
- Ask the children to practise spellings of words from high-frequency word list 1 – they could track these in the text, if they are included. Choose two or three of their words (such as *over, when, was*) to be class words of the week.

Extension/further reading

Make a class chart of the typical growth of a small child and make links to science work on life cycles and growth.

Following discussion of the features of non-fiction, ask the children to work in groups to sort a selection of books according to similar features, such as captions for pictures.

See How I Grow by Angela Wilkes (Dorling Kindersley) is a photographic record of the first 18 months of a baby's life.

1: 3: T18: to read recounts and begin to recognise generic structure, e.g. ordered sequence of events, use of words like *first, next, after, when*

How my body has changed

From a tiny baby to a schoolgirl, this is how I have grown.

First, as a baby only a few days old, I could only cry and drink milk.

The next thing I learned was to walk. I pushed a dog on wheels to help me.

When I was about six months old I could sit by myself without falling over. I could hold my toys.

When I was three years old I went to Nursery. I learned to ride a trike.

When I was nearly a year old I learned to crawl everywhere!

When I was five I started school. Then I learned to climb in PE.

focus is on physical development each time

sequencing words

events placed in order shows sequence of actions child able to do

each sentence shows age and actions

common irregular word

pictures help to explain text

1: 3: T20: to write simple recounts linked to topics of interest/study or to personal experience, using the language of texts read as models for own writing. Make group/class books, e.g. *our day at school, our trip to…*

1: 3: W7: to spell common irregular words from Appendix List 1

I came to Britain from Jamaica

by Valerie Fawcett

P 157

Background

This extract is taken from a book in the *Oxford Reading Tree Fact Finders* series which provides contrasting pictures of life in Jamaica and Britain, and describes a child's journey to Britain. The extract is a short recount of a child receiving a letter from her parents in Britain and then her plane journey to see them. It links with other recounts 'A first night away' (see page 100) and 'How my body has changed' (see page 102). It can form a useful model for writing recounts of journeys and also links with letter writing. The text can be used as a basis for a discussion about people not born in this country and the different places they are from.

Shared reading and discussing the text

- Begin by providing some background to the extract and talk about where Jamaica is, using a globe or map. If any of the children, or their parents, were born in countries other than Britain, talk about where they have come from. Use this as an opportunity to celebrate diversity, and if there are several children in the class from different countries, represent this in a class display.
- Now read the extract to the children, and discuss the child's journey. Ask the children how they think she felt – excited, scared? Make links with the children's own experiences of journeys.
- Read the extract again with the children; you might like to choose one child to read the letter.
- Now explain that, like other examples they have looked at, this is a recount that tells the order of events, in this case of a child's journey from Jamaica to Britain. Brainstorm the features of recounts and ask the children if they can remember if recounts tell what is happening now, or what happened in the past. List the main events in this recount.

Activities

- Ask the children to help you to list the sequence of events in the text, using sequencing words, such as *first, then, next, finally,* and tell the children that although the author did not use those words here, they can help to put events in the right order.
- Talk about letters and how we write them. Show the children one or two examples and look at the different layout of the letter. Talk about how letters always begin and end. Ask the children to write down some sample sentences.
- Model a written recount – it could be a letter – of a journey the children have experienced. Then provide the children with a writing frame and ensure that they have plenty of chance to rehearse orally sentences about their journey before writing them. Allow less able children to work with an adult to either scribe their recount, or record it on tape. Collect examples of recounts the children have written of journeys and make them into a class book for children to read.
- Work with the whole class or groups to practise spelling common words from Appendix List 1 that are contained in the text, such as *one* and *want*. Look carefully at the word together, highlight the tricky part and find a way of remembering it, then use the look, say, cover, write, check strategy.

Extension/further reading

Provide opportunities for letter writing in a range of contexts, for example letters to relatives whom the children do not see often, or letters written in a role-play area which has been made into an airport or a train station.

If you have a copy of the book, use it to compare pictures of schools in Jamaica with ones in Great Britain. Link this to work in geography on different places and the contrasts between hot and cold countries. In PSHE and citizenship, discuss living in a multicultural society.

Other titles in the *Oxford Reading Tree Fact Finders* series include *When Gran Was a Child* by Valerie Fawcett, and *All Kinds of Families* and *I Live in France* by John Foster (OUP).

1: 3: T18: to read recounts and begin to recognise generic structure, e.g. ordered sequence of events, use of words like first, next, after, when

I came to Britain from Jamaica

One day, I got a letter.
It was from my mum and dad.
They wanted me to come to Britain.

They sent me a picture.

I came to Britain on an aeroplane.

It took all night, and I had to sleep on the plane.

introduction/ orientation

'ed' ending used for past tense

common words for spelling

letter format

reader cannot see how letter ends

brief description of child's journey

1: 3: T20: to write simple recounts linked to topics of interest/study or to personal experience, using the language of texts read as models for own writing. Make group/class books, e.g. our day at school, our trip to…

1: 3: W7: to spell common irregular words from Appendix List 1

The House at Night by Stephen Webster

P 158

Background

This extract is from a book based on the 'Living and working together exhibition' at Eureka! The Museum for Children in Halifax. It describes what happens in a house at night and uses questions to promote discussion. It can be used as a good model for work on framing questions when looking at non-fiction texts in order to read with a clear purpose.

Shared reading and discussing the text

- Read the title to the children and show them the photographs. Ask them if they can predict the contents from the title and pictures.
- Now read the extract, then ask the children if they think it is from a story book (fiction) or gives us information (non-fiction). Contrast the opening of the extract with a fiction piece. Talk about the differences, using other examples of fiction and non-fiction.
- Read the extract again (using an enlarged version), with the children joining in. Ask them about the differences between their homes at night and in the day. Discuss the sequence of events when they go to bed. Talk about needing to feel safe at night and what people do to protect themselves. Encourage them to talk about their fears, such as fear of the dark.
- Explain that this extract describes the sequence of events at night as people go to bed. Deconstruct this by listing the sequence in order, for example *First, lock the doors; second, draw the curtains; third, switch off the lights.*
- Point to question marks in the text and highlight these with the children's help. Talk about why we use question marks and then underline the questions. Explain that it is good to think of questions when we are looking at non-fiction books as it gives us a reason for reading them.

Activities

- Focusing on the photographs, the children can work in pairs, with one child asking a question based on a picture and the other answering it.
- Provide the children with copies of the text on which you have highlighted or underlined the questions. Ask them to work in pairs to write suitable answers.
- Give the children a sample of text, taken from the extract, with the question marks missing. Ask them to put in the missing question marks.
- Contrast a human being's pattern of sleeping with that of nocturnal animals. Draw up a list of nocturnal animals. Encourage the children to write questions for other members of the class to answer, such as *Which animals like to go out at night?* Model writing answers for the class to see.

Extension/further reading

Provide the children with different questions on card (one per card), with the answers on separate cards, and ask them to match the questions to the answers. For example, ask them to match a question on houses to a suitable card, a question on families to a suitable card, and so on.

Ask more able children to devise their own questions based on the contents of a non-fiction book. For a book on plants, for example, they could ask: *What are roots of plants for?*

Compare this extract with another non-fiction text on houses and homes, looking closely at the information it contains.

Make a class non-fiction book on homes, with different sections for different rooms in the house.

Link the extract to work in geography on comparing homes – detached, semi-detached, terraced, cottage, and so on – and list the typical features of each. Follow this up by asking the children to match a description with a type of house.

In art and design, make night-time pictures of shapes and shadows, using black sugar paper outlines on lighter paper.

Further reading includes *Homes* by Teresa Heapy from the *Discovery World* series (Heinemann).

1: 3: T17: to recognise that non-fiction books on similar themes can give different information and present similar information in different ways

The House at Night

Everybody needs to feel warm and safe before they go to sleep, and so does the house. The grown-ups lock the doors, draw the curtains and switch everything off. How do you prepare for sleep? Probably first of all you change into your night-clothes, brush your teeth and say goodnight. Do you have a bedtime story, a favourite toy or a night light? Are there things you like to think about, just before going to sleep?

Lights make us forget the dark outside. How do you feel when the lights go out and everything looks different?

At night other animals are quite active. Minibeasts crawl out of their hiding places and search for food. Cats like to hunt and explore but a dog is happier to sleep and dream.

opening to non-fiction text

question mark at end of each question

procedure at night – tasks to be done before going to bed

questions to reader

contrasts with humans

this paragraph the only one without a question

1: 3: T22: to write own questions prior to reading for information and to record answers, e.g. as lists, a completed chart, extended captions for display, a fact file on IT

1: 3: S7: to add question marks to questions

Animal senses

P 159

Background

This extract illustrates how information in non-fiction books is gleaned from pictures and text, and contains a range of interesting facts about animal senses. It provides a stimulus for children to devise their own questions – an essential skill for information retrieval.

This follows on from work on questioning in 'The House at Night' (see page 106) and it also links with 'Minibeast Movements' (see page 30), 'Animal lists' (see page 40), 'A minibeast' (see page 70) and 'Duckling' (see page 72).

Shared reading and discussing the text

- Begin by talking about the senses and ensure that the children can name all five. Now go on to give some background information about how some animals use certain senses in rather strange ways. Bats, for example, use their hearing in a similar way to our use of sight.
- Now read the extract, pausing to look at the pictures with the children. Explain that non-fiction books can give us amazing information, both from the words and the pictures. If possible, look at another example of a text about animals, particularly if it includes some of the animals mentioned in this extract.
- Read the text again, with the children joining in. Pause over unfamiliar words (*bloodhounds, microscopic, fennec,* and so on) and model using different strategies to read them, for example sounding the words out (*f-e-nn-e-c*). Use words from the extract to instigate a collection of animal names for display in the classroom.
- Discuss the different animals and how they use senses differently. Draw up a chart of the animals mentioned here and the particular heightened senses they illustrate; then go on to add to these in later work using other non-fiction texts.
- Model using a KWL grid, beginning with the first two columns (*What do I Know? What do I Want to know?*). Write appropriate information in each column, for example *I know that dogs have a strong sense of smell; I want to know which other animals have a strong sense of smell.* This process will help the children to formulate more precise questions.

Activities

- Ask the children to fill in their KWL grids, beginning with the first two columns, as you have modelled, for information they already know and further facts they want to find out. Write examples of questions together that the text provides the answers to, such as *What do flies taste with?* or *What do sharks use to find food?* The children can then write down questions on their KWL grids. Revise work on question marks and remind the children to ensure they add a question mark each time.
- Look at the text to find answers to the questions and let the children complete the last column of their grids (*What have I Learned?*). Point out that scanning for a particular word is helpful, such as *feet* when looking for the answer to the question *What sense do flies use with their feet?*
- Reinforce the above activities by providing a range of questions that relate to this extract for the children to answer in plenary sessions.

Extension/further reading

Encourage the children to devise their own questions on different animals (for example, *How do bats find their way in the dark?*) and use information texts, CD-ROMs or the Internet to find the answers. Draw attention to features of non-fiction books, such as headings, contents lists and indexes, which can be used to help them to find answers to specific questions.

Link the activities to science work on senses and animals and make a classroom display entitled 'Some amazing facts about animals'.

Further reading includes *In the Country* by Karen Bryant-Mole (Heinemann Library).

1: 3: T19: to identify simple questions and use text to find answers. To locate parts of text that give particular information including labelled diagrams and charts, e.g. *parts of a car, what pets eat, clothes that keep us warm.*

ANIMAL SENSES

Animals use their senses – touch, smell, taste, sight and hearing to find out about the world around them.

Here are some amazing things that animals can do:

FLIES HAVE TASTE sensors on their feet, to test food when they land on it.

A DOG USES its sense of smell to find out all kinds of information. Bloodhounds can even detect the microscopic pieces of skin that are shed from a moving person's body.

SOME SNAKES CAN feel the heat rays from animals they want to eat, like mice. They use their tongues to taste smells in the air.

A FENNEC FOX'S huge ears help it to hear danger or find food to eat. The fennec fox can hear a desert beetle kicking over sand grains many metres away.

A SHARK CAN smell blood in the water hundreds of metres away.

CRICKETS HAVE EARS on their knees which help them to hear their mates.

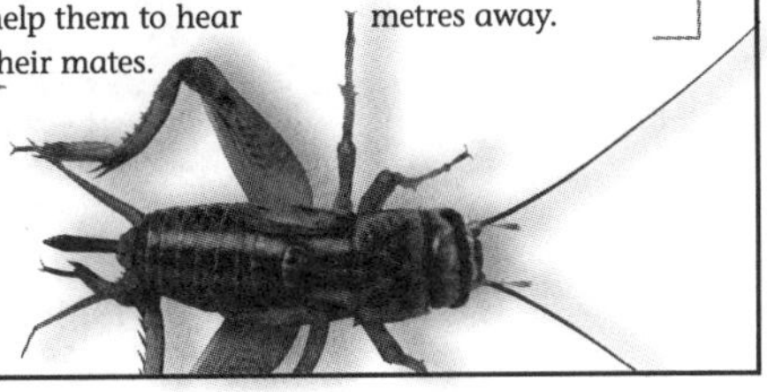

tells us that the topic is about senses

text explains picture of dog

unfamiliar words

sharks use their sense of smell to find food

snakes use their sense of taste to find food

a type of fox

this fox has heightened hearing sense

text tells reader unusual facts

1: 3: T22: to write own questions prior to reading for information and to record answers, e.g. as lists, a completed chart, extended captions for display, a fact file on IT

1: 3: S7: to add question marks to questions

1: 3: W8: to gather new words from reading and shared experiences, and to make collections of personal interest or significant words and words linked to particular topics

The Tiger who came to tea

Sophie opened
the door, and
there was a big,
furry,
stripy tiger.
The tiger said,
"Excuse me, but
I'm very hungry.
Do you think
I could have
tea with you?"
Sophie's mummy
said, "Of course,
come in."

Judith Kerr

Lucy's Picture

Lucy started her picture. She cut some soft green velvet into curvy mounds, like hills, and stuck them on the paper. She made a lake out of blue shiny stuff, and put it in between the hills. Then she found some flowery dress material.

"Grandpa has flowers like this in his garden," Lucy told Mrs Kelly. "He likes the blue ones best because they have the nicest smell." She cut round the flowers and stuck them in little clumps along the edge of the lake.

At playtime Lucy was too busy to play. Instead she collected twigs and leaves and then she found two small feathers! She filled her empty juice cup with sand from the sandpit. At last it was time to go inside.

Now Lucy was very excited about Grandpa's picture. She made him a tree out of the twigs and the leaves, and stuck the feathers on the end of a branch. Then she spread some glue in a long winding band over the hills, and scattered sand over the glue to make a path.

Nicola Moon

Tell Me What It's Like to Be Big

"Tell me what it's like to be big," said Willa.

"You can do lots of things," said Willoughby.

"What things?"

"You'll be able to reach the lamp by yourself when you're big," said Willoughby.

"Will I?" said Willa.

"Oh yes," said Willoughby. "And when you're really big, nearly as big as I'll be, you might be able to reach the moon in a rocket!"

"What else will I do when I'm big?" asked Willa.

"You'll be able to stand in the shower like me and turn it on by yourself," said Willoughby.

"Will I?" said Willa.

"You'll be able to reach for a towel and get dried by yourself," said Willoughby.

"Will I?" said Willa.

"And you'll be able to brush your own teeth without any help," said Willoughby.

"And will Spotty Ted brush his?" asked Willa.

"He hasn't got any teeth," said Willoughby.

Joyce Dunbar

What Can I Write? Rosie Writes Again

Rosie's teacher has asked the class to write a story about what they did in the holidays. Rosie can't think of a single thing. She hadn't been anywhere. She hadn't done anything.

She asked, "What can I write?"

Miss West said, "Come on, Rosie, just start!"

The first day of my holiday Mum was working. I had to go to Mrs Benn's next door. I don't like Mrs Benn much and I didn't like what she cooked for lunch. It was horrible liver and onions and cabbage. I wouldn't eat it.

Mrs Benn said, "Children today don't know what's good for them."

She gave it to her cat Lilly and I had a cheese sandwich. Afterwards I played with Lilly while Mrs Benn was knitting. Lilly got the wool in a terrible mess!

When Mum came back to get me she promised we'd go to the Toy Museum next day.

Martina Selway

Where Are You, Blue Kangaroo?

Blue Kangaroo belonged to Lily.
He was her very own kangaroo.
Sometimes Blue Kangaroo disappeared and Lily would say,
"Where are you, Blue Kangaroo?"
And Blue Kangaroo waited for Lily to find him.

One day, Lily's friend, Florence, took Lily to the park.
"Hold tight to Blue Kangaroo," said Florence.

Lily swung on the swings, and she wasn't scared on the slide.

"I love ice-cream!" said Lily...

...and Blue Kangaroo wondered if Lily had forgotten him.

As they were leaving, Lily suddenly shrieked,
"Where are you, Blue Kangaroo?"
"Did you leave him on the slide?" asked Florence.

"Here he is!" smiled Lily.
"You must try to be more careful," said Florence.

The next Saturday, Lily's Aunt Jemima took Lily shopping.
"Hold tight to Blue Kangaroo," said Aunt Jemima.

Emma Chichester Clark

It's the Bear!

"A bear?" said Mum. "That's
silly, dear!
We don't get great big bears
round here."

"There's just you and me and
your teddy, Freddy.
Now let's all get the picnic
ready."

"We've got lettuce,
tomatoes,
creamy cheese spread,
with hard-boiled eggs
and crusty brown bread.
There's orange juice,
biscuits,
some crisps and –

OH MY!

I've forgotten to pack
the blueberry pie..."

"I'll pop back and get it,"
she said. "Won't be long."

"BUT MUM!"
gasped Eddy...

too late –
SHE HAD GONE!

He sat on the hamper
and tried not to cry,
then...

"I CAN SMELL FOOD!"
yelled a voice
from nearby.

"IT'S THE BEAR!"
cried Eddy.
"WHERE CAN I HIDE?"

Then he opened
the hamper and
clambered inside.

Out of the trees
stepped a big hungry bear,
licking his lips
and sniffing the air.

Jez Alborough

SUMMER RAIN

Who felt the rain begin?
I, said the bat.
Safe, in my secret skin,
darting now out, now in,
I felt the rain begin.
I, said the bat.

Who heard the shower fall?
I, said the snail.
High on the garden wall
I heard it splash and fall –
summer rain over all.
I, said the snail.

Who sipped it, drop by drop?
I, said the bird.
I hoped it wouldn't stop!
Hurrying, hop-hop-hop –
I drank it, drop by drop.
I, said the bird.

Jean Kenward

Follow My Leader!

Over the stile,
Leaping and bounding,
Follow my leader!

Up the hill,
Puffing and panting,
Follow my leader!

Round the corner,
Jumping and jiving,
Follow my leader!

Down the steps,
Bumping and thumping,
Follow my leader!

Across the stream,
Splishing and splashing,
Follow my leader!

Into the woods,
Shouting and roaring,
Follow my leader!

But wait...
Can you hear it?
Shhh! What's that noise?

RRROOOAAAR!

"I want to play,"
The tiger said, smiling.

Emma Chichester Clark

Who Likes Cornflakes?

Who likes cornflakes?
Who likes beans?
Who likes pizza?
Who likes greens?
Who likes apples?
Who likes cheese?
Who likes pudding?
Who likes peas?
Who likes ice cream
for their tea?
  Grandma,
    Mum,
      and
        Dad,
          and
            Me!

Wes Magee

Seeds

Seeds that twist and seeds that twirl
Seeds with wings which spin and whirl;

Seeds that float on thistledown
Seeds in coats of glossy brown;

Seeds that burst with popping sound
From their pods to reach the ground;

Seeds with hooks that clutch and cling
Seeds I plant for flowers next spring.

Hilda I Rostron

MINIBEAST MOVEMENTS

This is the way
the beetle stumbles,
clumsy, clockwork, slow.

This is the way
the grasshopper leaps,
so, so, so!

This is the way
the snail slides,
smooth, steady, sure.

And this is the way
the spider scuttles
swiftly across the floor.

Tony Mitton

What's in Your Pocket, Lucy Locket?

What's in your pocket,
Lucy Locket?

Just another pocket
Tied with a bow
Let's go and ask
Pinocchio.

What's in your pocket,
Pinocchio?

Only some plays
And a couple of puppets.
Let's go and ask
Little Miss Muffet.

What's in your pocket,
Little Miss Muffet?

Yuck! A dead spider
And a cookery book.
Let's go and ask
Captain Hook.

What's in your pocket,
Captain Hook?

Paul and Emma Rogers

RULES FOR THE CLOAKROOM

Please:

Hang your coat on a peg.

Put your shoes under the bench.

Put your gloves or mittens in your coat pocket.

Put your hat on a peg.

Hang your bag on a peg.

Leave the cloakroom tidy.

Put any litter in the big bin.

David Waugh

Plan of a school

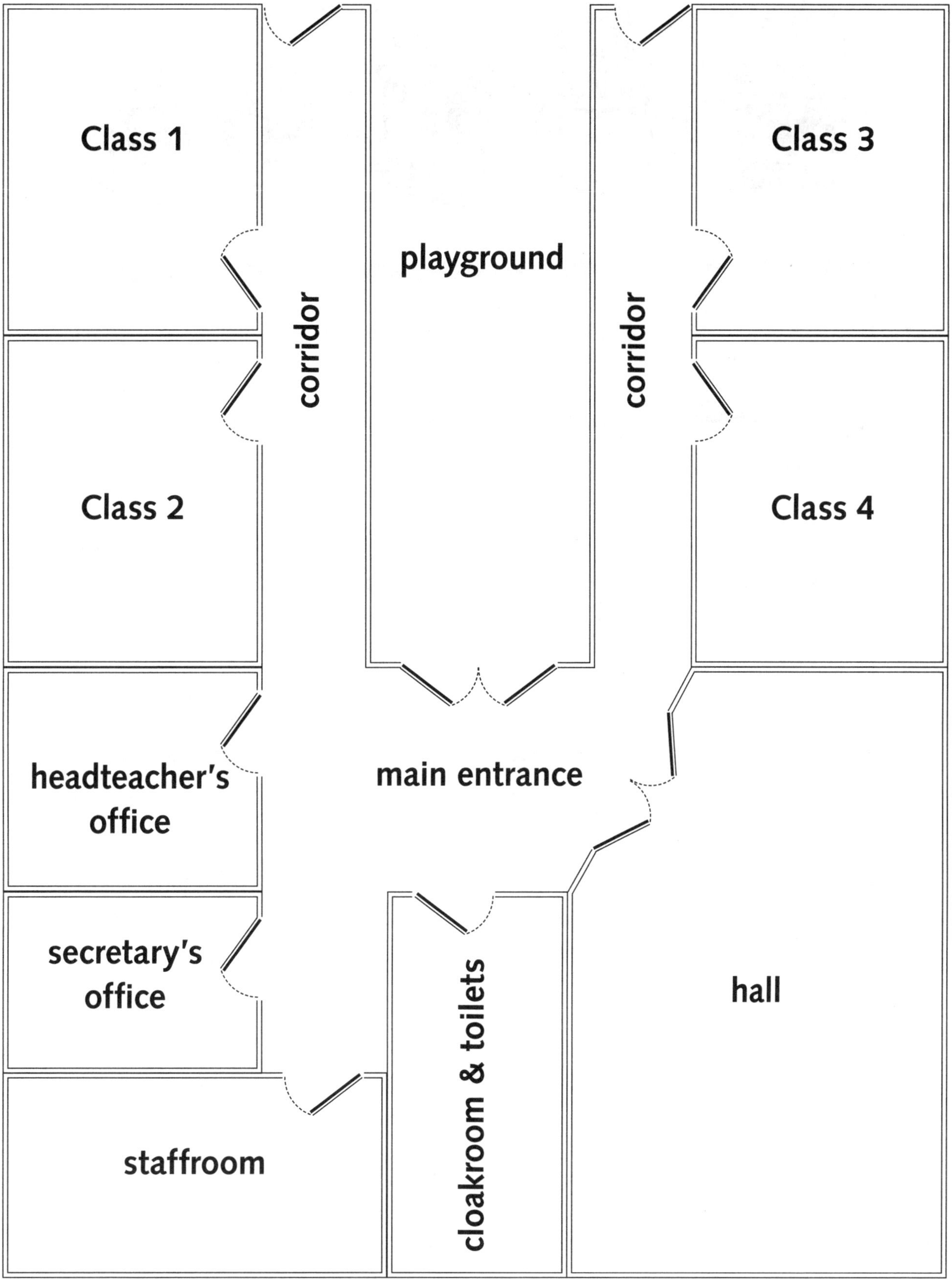

David Waugh

Labelled drawers

David Waugh

Animal lists

Pets

dog

cat

guinea pig

hamster

Farm animals

cow

pig

horse

hen

Wild animals

deer

squirrel

stoat

hare

In which list does each of these animals belong?

Some may belong in more than one list.

rabbit

fox

sheep

mouse

rat

bull

David Waugh

Make a list

Things to do

Remember PE kit

Remember dinner money

Take apple to teacher

Things to do

Pack case

Remember tickets

Lock doors

Things to do

Put cat out

Empty bin

Lock shed

Father Christmas list

computer game

video

dressing-up clothes

drawing set

book of magic tricks

magic conjuring set

Plasticine

play tent

Shopping list

bread

yogurt

cheese

spaghetti

milk

butter

jam

cornflakes

sugar

David Waugh

Little Red Riding Hood

One fine afternoon in August, the little girl's mum packed some of Grandma's favourite things in a bag: some homemade tarts and pickles, a bottle of stout, and the paper with the weekend television programmes in it. Little Red Riding Hood set off on her weekly visit to Grandma's house. Her parents walked down to the bottom of the field with her.

"Hurry straight to Grandma's," they called, waving goodbye.

"Don't play about on the way, and don't lose yourself in daydreams!"

Retold by Tony Ross

The Frog Prince

Many years ago there lived a King and Queen who had an only daughter. She was very beautiful and loved playing with her friends in the royal park, which was full of splendid trees and sparkling fountains.

One day she took her friends out to play a game with her favourite golden ball. Once the lovely golden ball was just about to drop into the Princess's hands when suddenly the sun got in her eyes. The ball dropped to her feet and rolled swiftly into a well near by. The Princess ran forward and bent over the well, heartbroken to see her golden ball disappear into the dark green waters. She began to weep and when her friends tried to cheer her up she sent them away and just sat there alone, all sad and tear-stained.

Suddenly she heard a little croaking voice saying:

"What is the matter, little princess? Why is so beautiful a girl so sad?"

"Oh, froggie," she replied. "I am crying because my golden ball has fallen into the well."

"Never mind," said the frog, "I can easily dive down and fetch it up again."

"Can you really?" said the Princess. "Please do. I shall give you anything you wish to have if you bring me back my golden ball! Even my golden crown!"

"I do not want your crown," replied the frog gravely. "All I want is to sit by you and eat at your table, drink from your cup and sleep in your bed."

Retold by Stephen Corrin

The Three Wishes

Extract 1

Long, long ago in a forest a voice could be heard.

"Trees, trees, trees," said the voice grumpily. "Chop, chop, chop, saw, saw, saw. All day long, every day, that's all I do."

The voice belonged to a woodcutter who lived with his wife in a little house next to a forest. The woodcutter worked hard all day cutting down trees. He sawed branches into logs for people to burn on their fires. He sawed the trunks of the trees into planks which could be used to make furniture. In fact, he cut down so many that there were spaces in the forest without any trees at all.

One evening, as he sat wearily in his chair after another hard day's work, the woodcutter said to his wife, "I'm sick of trees, trees, trees, chopping, chopping, chopping and sawing, sawing, sawing!"

His wife said, "Do stop grumbling, and I wish you wouldn't say everything three times when you're cross. It could be a lot worse. Some people don't have jobs or homes to live in."

But the woodcutter was not happy and every day he grumbled when he had to go to work and grumbled again when he got home. He grumbled while he was working, even though he was alone and no one could hear him. "Trees, trees, trees," he would mutter, "I'm sick of cutting them down and cutting them up."

One day he was sitting on the stump of a tree which he had just chopped down, grumbling to himself about how hard his life was. Suddenly, he heard someone say, "Please don't cut any more trees down. The forest is disappearing and the birds and animals will soon have nowhere to live."

The woodcutter looked around and there, standing next to an oak tree, was a tiny man.

"I have to cut down the trees because if I don't my wife and I will not have enough money to buy food," he said to the little man, who was dressed all in green with a green pointed hat on his head.

The tiny man looked up at the woodcutter and pleaded, "Please don't cut any more trees down unless you plant some in their place. If you promise to do that, I will grant you three wishes."

"Three wishes?" said the woodcutter. "Now that sounds like a good thing. All right, I won't cut any more trees down."

"You have to make the wishes in your house or they won't work," the little man told him before he vanished.

The woodcutter could not wait to get home to make his wishes. He hurried through the woods and burst into the house, eager to tell his wife what had happened.

Retold by David Waugh

The Three Wishes

Extract 2

"Where's the wood for the fire?" asked the woodcutter's wife as he came in.

"I haven't brought any," replied the woodcutter, "but it's all right, I'll never need to cut wood again. You see, I met a little man in the woods and he told me that if I didn't cut any more trees down, he'd grant me three wishes. We're going to be rich!" And the woodcutter took his wife in his arms and tried to dance with her.

"Get off me, you stupid man!" she cried. "How can you be so daft? We need wood for the fire so that I can cook supper, but you haven't brought any. All you have managed to do is make up some silly story as an excuse for not doing your job. Well, I'm not making you any supper!"

The woodcutter decided it was not worth arguing with his wife so he sat in his chair and sulked instead. When supper time came he sat and watched as she ate bread and cheese without offering him any. He felt very hungry indeed.

"Oh I wish I had a string of tasty sausages!" he said, and suddenly he had. A string of sausages lay on his lap. His wife was furious.

"So you did have three wishes," she said. "Well what a stupid waste of a wish to ask for sausages. I wish they had landed on your nose!"

With that, the sausages flew through the air and stuck to the woodcutter's nose.

"So my wishes come true too," she said as her husband begged her to help get the sausages off his nose. They both pulled and pulled, but the sausages were stuck.

Finally, the woodcutter said, "Sausages, sausages, sausages! I wish they would disappear," and sure enough they did in a flash.

The woodcutter and his wife were sad that they had wasted their three wishes and had nothing to show for them, but as the days passed they began to see the funny side of what had happened. Whenever they thought about the sausages stuck on the end of the woodcutter's nose, they laughed until they cried. In fact, they were happier than they had ever been, and the woodcutter stopped saying things three times, worked hard at his job and took care never to cut down trees without planting others in their place.

Retold by David Waugh

The Tortoise and the Hare

"You are so slo-o-o-w!" said Hare as he watched Tortoise ambling along the road.

"I get to where I want to go soon enough," said Tortoise. "Sometimes you can get to places more quickly without rushing."

"Well you won't ever get anywhere quicker than me," boasted Hare.

"You might be surprised," said Tortoise slowly.

"So, do you think you can beat me in a race?" asked Hare.

"Maybe," mumbled Tortoise, "maybe."

"Right, we'll have a race," said Hare, "and I'll beat you easily."

So Hare and Tortoise went to see Fox and asked him to make a start and a finishing line for the race. Then the two animals stood at the starting line waiting for Fox to say "Ready, Steady, Go!" As soon as he did, Hare dashed off towards the woods while Tortoise plodded along the path in his usual steady way.

After a few minutes, Hare thought that he would stop and have a rest. Tortoise will take hours to get to the finishing line, he thought. I'll sit under a shady tree and wait until he catches up and then I'll run to the finishing line and win the race.

But Hare began to get drowsy as he lay in the shade of the tree and he soon fell asleep. After about an hour, Tortoise walked slowly past him without waking him and went along the path towards the finishing line. When Hare woke up he rubbed his eyes and remembered the race. He rushed along the path as fast as his legs would carry him, but, by the time he reached the finishing line, Tortoise had already won the race and was sitting under a shady tree waiting for him.

"I told you," he said, "I get to where I want to go soon enough. Sometimes you can get to places more quickly without rushing."

Retold by David Waugh

The Three Little Pigs

The first little pig in a house of straw
heard a tap tap tap on her little green door.
"Little pig, little pig, let me come in,"
said the big bad wolf with a big bad grin.
Then he huffed and he puffed and he huffed some more
and down went the little pig's house of straw.
The next little pig was taking a nap
in her house of sticks when she heard a tap
and the big bad wolf with a big bad grin
gave a huff and a puff and blew her house in.
Then the big bad wolf, still up to his tricks,
went off to the third little house of bricks.
"Little pig, little pig, let me come in,"
said the big bad wolf with a big bad grin.
And he huffed and he puffed till his face turned red.
"My house is too tough," the little pig said.
"I'll come down the chimney," the wolf yelled, "Now!"
But the fire was lit and the wolf yelled, "Ow!"
and shot straight out in a cloud of smoke
as the third little pig gave the fire a poke.
The wolf blew on his paws with a huff and a puff
and he hobbled off home. He'd had enough.

Marian Swinger

Half a Moon and One Whole Star

Up above the earth so far
Hang half a moon and one whole star
Hang one whole star and half a moon:
Night-time will be coming soon.
But where there's night there's day to follow
Sleep Susan sleep, for come tomorrow
Above the earth there will be one
Hotly glowing summer sun
Round and orange, like a ball
Like moon and star, you'll have them all!
So sleep, Susan, sleep.

Crescent Dragonwagon

WEATHER

Dot a dot dot dot a dot dot
Spotting the windowpane.
Spack a spack speck flick a flack fleck
Freckling the windowpane.

A spatter a scatter a wet cat a clatter
A splatter a rumble outside.
Umbrella umbrella umbrella umbrella
Bumbershoot barrel of rain.

Slosh a galosh slosh a galosh
Slither and slather a glide
A puddle a jump a puddle a jump
A puddle a pump aluddle a dump a
Puddmuddle jump in and slide!

Eve Merriam

Whose is it?

Characters

Two children.

Production notes

The two speakers in this dialogue are arguing over an unspecified object.

A: This is my one!

B: No, it's not!

A: It is! It's the one I got!

B: No, it isn't – look here! See…

A: It's the one that was given to me.

B: It isn't yours: I can show…

A: It's mine! It is! I know!

B: Don't pull – it's not very strong!

A: I want it. I'm right – you're wrong.

B: It's yours. Look: it's broken in two.

A: It's not mine: it belongs to you.

Charles Thomson

From seed to sunflower

In autumn the seeds of fully grown sunflowers fall to the ground. A seed contains the tiny plant and the food the plant will need before it starts to grow.

The seeds are buried in the soil. The soil contains minerals. Minerals are special foods that help the plant to grow. In spring the warm sun and rain make the seeds begin to grow.
This is called germination.

Sunflower words

Germination
The stage in the life cycle of a plant when the seeds first begin to grow.

Minerals
Special food in the soil. Plants need minerals to help them grow.

Dr Gerald Legg

Keeping fit

When you **exercise**, you use many different parts of your body. Regular exercise keeps you fit and healthy.

Exercising makes your **heart** and **lungs** work hard, and this makes them strong.

Paul Bennett

Hearing

Sounds travel through the air but you can't see them.

You use your ears to hear them.

The outer part of your ear catches the sounds and sends them down a hole. This hole leads to a tunnel that goes right inside your ear.

At the end of the tunnel there is a thin bit of skin. This is stretched tight across the end of the tunnel, just like the skin on the top of a drum.

This is called your ear-drum.

Mandy Suhr; illustration Mike Gordon

Weather: rain

What is rain?

Rain is water that falls from the sky as raindrops. Some parts of the world may have rain all year round. **Deserts** have little or no rain.

Clouds, hail and fog

If raindrops travel high up in the clouds where it is very cold, they freeze. They fall as balls of ice called **hailstones**. If you cut a hailstone in half you can see the layers of ice.

Rain fact

Light rain made up of small raindrops is called drizzle.

Jillian Powell

A MINIBEAST

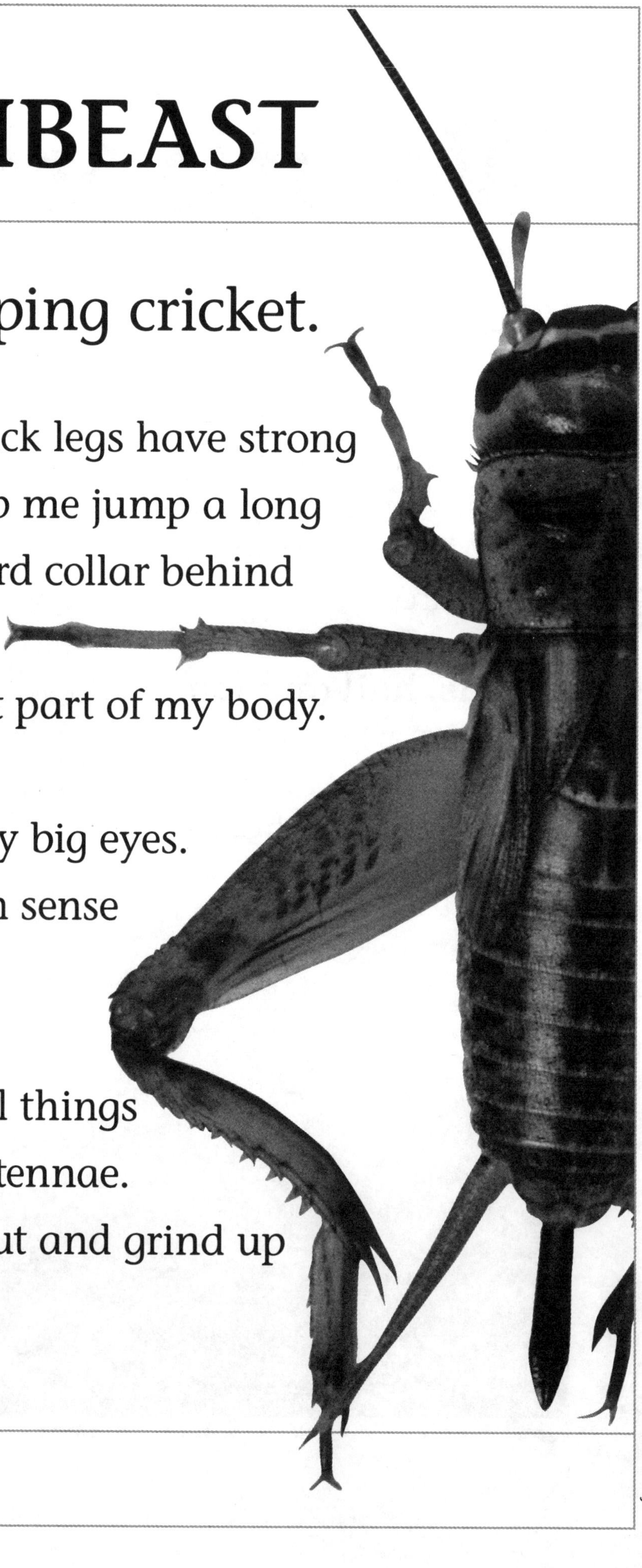

I am a jumping cricket.

My enormous back legs have strong muscles that help me jump a long way. I have a hard collar behind my head that protects the front part of my body.

I see well with my big eyes. My front legs can sense sounds.

I touch and smell things with my long antennae. My biting jaws cut and grind up my food.

Barbara Taylor

Duckling

Ducklings hatch from eggs. Soon after hatching, they follow the mother duck to the pond to find food.

These ducklings are just one day old. In a few weeks they will lose their soft down and grow feathers.

Angela Royston

Healthy eating

You need food to help your body grow and to give you energy. Different sorts of food help to keep you healthy. That is why it is important to eat a balanced diet. This means that you should eat different types of food every day so that you get all the nutrients your body needs.

Different foods help your body in different ways.

Growth and repair

Protein foods help you to grow by feeding your muscles, skin and bones.

Which of these foods do you like to eat? You should eat some of these foods every day as proteins also help your body to repair itself when it gets injured.

Food for energy

You can help to give your body energy by eating foods that contain carbohydrates.

Carbohydrates can be found in these foods.

When you run about at playtime and exercise in PE lessons you use up lots of energy. You even use energy when you are asleep!

Carbohydrates can also be found in sugary foods such as jam, cakes and chocolate. Do you think these foods can help you to stay healthy?

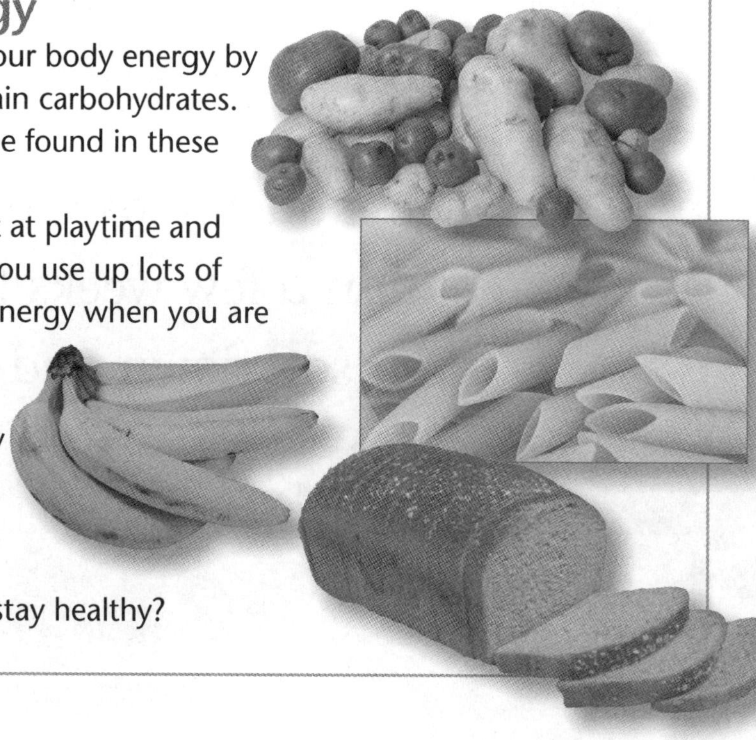

Claire Head

Satoshi Kitamura

Anthony Browne

Through the Magic Mirror

He was out in the street.

It seemed like the same old street, but was it?

Falling Angels

The first time Sally flew was before she could even crawl. As her parents slept, she floated above them, too young to speak, too young to think in words.

The first time Sally saw someone else flying, she was seven. Her mother was sleeping in the warm summer afternoon. Beside her in the grass her baby brother Peter curled up in her shadow. As Sally floated over the garden, she saw the baby stretch out and rise into the air.

Maybe it's just us, she thought, something special about our family.

As the years passed, Sally flew to wild and wonderful places, distant lands she had only seen in books. And in the afternoons she sat by her grandmother's bed and told her about everything she'd seen.

"You and your silly stories," said her mother. "It's time you came down to earth."

"They're not stories," said Sally when her mother had left the room.

Her grandmother just smiled.

I'll prove it, said Sally to herself, and the next morning, while everyone was still asleep, she flew into the heart of Africa. She watched the sun creep over the horizon and wake up the world for another day. She flew into the deepest part of the rainforest and in the branches of a great firewheel tree she found a beautiful orchid, which she took back to her grandmother.

Colin Thompson

The Brave Little Grork

This is a **grork**.
Grorks are shy and easily frightened.

This is a **greep**.
Greeps are not shy and they hardly ever get frightened.

One day the greep wanted to go to the wood. He waited patiently while the grork got ready. This took a long time.

"Thinking brave thoughts works," he said, very excited. "It really does."

"It works for me too," the greep said.

But suddenly, there they were by the haunted tree. The grork had heard that an old crow who'd been struck by lightning swooped down from its branches on stormy nights.

The grork felt small and frightened. Before he could think brave thoughts, the wind blew and the branches

cree-ee-eaked!

"Run," cried the grork.
"Run for your life."

Kathryn Cave; illustrations Nick Maland

Porwigles

Six porwigles
Wriggling in a pool,
Pretending to be whales
And trying to keep cool.
One porwigle whale
Tried a flying dive—
When they had a tail count
There were only five.

Five porwigles
Wriggling in a pool,
Pretending to be whales
And trying to keep cool.
One porwigle whale
Went off to explore—
When they had a tail count
There were only four.

Four porwigles
Wriggling in a pool,
Pretending to be whales
And trying to keep cool.
One porwigle whale
Went to find the sea—
When they had a tail count
There were only three.

Three porwigles
Wriggling in a pool,
Pretending to be whales
And trying to keep cool.
One porwigle whale
Didn't like the view—
When they had a tail count
There were only two.

Two porwigles
Wriggling in a pool,
Pretending to be whales
And trying to keep cool.
One porwigle whale
Went to see his Mum—
Left the last one on his own,
There is only one.

One porwigle
Wriggling in a pool,
Feeling rather lonely
And trying to keep cool.
One all alone porwigle
Jumped onto a log—
And you couldn't count *his* tail
Because he's turned into a frog!

Julie Holder

(Porwigle is an old English name for a tadpole.)

Here is the Nose

Here is the Nose that smelled something sweet
And led the search for a bite to eat.

Here are the Feet that followed the Nose
Around the kitchen on ten Tiptoes.

Here are the Eyes that looked high and low
Till they spotted six pans sitting all in a row.

Here are the Arms that reached up high
To bring down a fresh-baked blueberry pie.

Here is the Mouth that opened up wide.
Here are the Hands that put pie inside.

Here is the Tongue that licked the tin
And lapped up the juice running down the Chin.

Here is the Stomach that growled for more.
Here are the Legs that ran for the door.

Here are the Ears that heard a whack.
Here is the Bottom that felt a smack!

Clyde Watson

There Was an Old Woman

There was an old woman of Chester-le-Street
Who chased a policeman all over his beat.

She shattered his helmet and tattered his clothes
And knocked his new spectacles clean off his nose.

"I'm afraid," said the Judge, "I must make it quite clear
You can't get away with that sort of thing here."

"I can and I will," the old woman she said,
"And I don't give a fig for your water and bread.

"I don't give a hoot for your cold prison cell,
And your bolts and your bars and your handcuffs as well.

"I've never been one to do just as I'm bid.
You can put me in jail for a year!"
So they did.

Charles Causley

When the Wind Blows

When the wind blows
Coats flap, scarves flutter.

When the wind blows
Branches groan, leaves mutter.

When the wind blows
Curtains swish, papers scatter.

When the wind blows
Gates creak, dustbins clatter.

When the wind blows
Doors slam, windows rattle.

When the wind blows
Inside is a haven,
Outside is a battle.

John Foster

THE MARCH WIND

I come to work as well as play;
I'll tell you what I do;
I whistle all the livelong day,
"Woo-oo-oo-oo! Woo-oo!"
I toss the branches up and down
And shake them to and fro,
I whirl the leaves in flocks of brown,
And send them high and low.
I strew the twigs upon the ground,
The frozen earth I sweep;
I blow the children round and round
And wake the flowers from sleep.

Anonymous

THE SOUND OF THE WIND

The wind has such a rainy sound
Moaning through the town,
The sea has such a windy sound –
Will the ships go down?

The apples in the orchard
Tumble from their tree –
Oh will the ships go down, go down,
In the windy sea?

Christina Rossetti

When I'm Big

When I'm big, I'm going to stay up as late as I like and make myself marshmallows on toast instead of going to bed.

When I'm big, I'm going swimming with the whales in the deep blue sea instead of puddling about in the bath.

When I'm big, I'm going to wear a bird-suit and gumboots all day long instead of a jumper and dungarees.

When I'm big, I'm going to have a huge back garden with sand mountains that touch the sky and a lake in the middle instead of a sandpit and a paddling pool.

When I'm big, I'm going to drive the trolley round the shops with Dad in it instead of the other way round.

When I'm big, I'm going to grow triffids and Venus fly-traps and man-eating orchids instead of mustard and cress.

Debi Gliori

But Martin!

That first morning back at school
Lee's lips turned down
Lloyd's head hung down
Billy's brows drew down
And Angela's tears fell down
but that was before they found
MARTIN!

Lee's face was smooth and golden
Lloyd's face was round and brown
Billy's face was square and red
And Angela's face was long and white
but Martin's face was
GREEN!

Lee's hair was black and silky
Lloyd's hair was black and bouncy
Billy's hair was red and spiky
And Angela's hair was fair and floaty
but Martin's hair
WASN'T THERE!
(he just had these)

When they saw him
Lee giggled
Lloyd shouted
Billy whistled
and Angela gasped
but Martin
BLEEPED!

Then they began to play.
Lee skipped
Billy chased
Lloyd jumped
and Angela cartwheeled
but Martin
FLOATED!

The bell rang and
Lee stood still
Lloyd stopped dead
Billy wobbled
and Angela froze
but Martin
VANISHED!

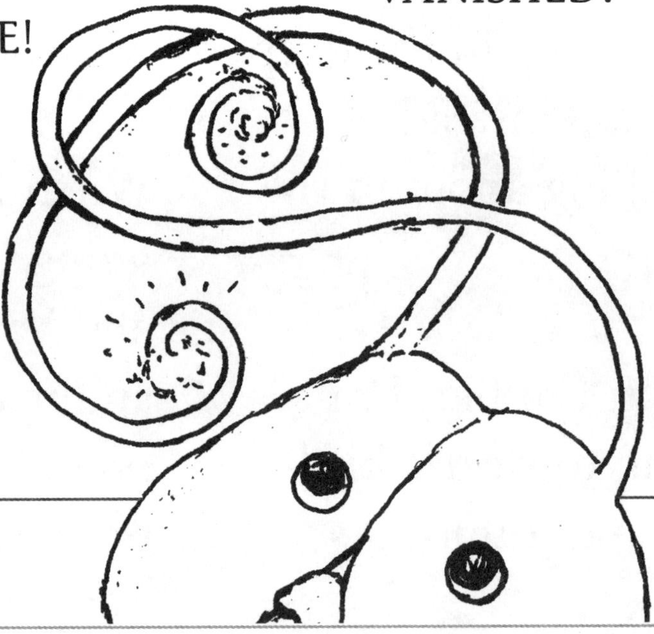

A first night away

Going to stay away from home for the first time can be very exciting. This is what happened when Sam, a five-year-old boy, went to stay with his best friend, Tom.

First, Sam packed his pyjamas and clean clothes in a bag. Next, he packed a few toys, not forgetting his teddy. Then it was time to go. Sam's mum drove him to Tom's house, and Sam went to play with Tom in his bedroom.

Sam spent a good day with his friend. In the afternoon they had a trip to the park. They each had an ice cream. When they went back to Tom's house there was time to play with Tom's toys and watch TV. Then they ate their tea together. After that, they had fun in the bath together.

Later at bedtime, Sam began to miss home. Tom's mum read them a bedtime story and gave them both a goodnight kiss. But Sam couldn't get to sleep and finally went downstairs. He felt very sad, so his mum had to come and fetch him. He was wrapped up in a blanket and taken home to his own bed. Sam was disappointed that he did not stay the night at his friend's house, but perhaps he will when he is bigger.

Wendy Jolliffe

How my body has changed

From a tiny baby to a schoolgirl, this is how I have grown.

First, as a baby only a few days old, I could only cry and drink milk.

The next thing I learned was to walk. I pushed a dog on wheels to help me.

When I was about six months old I could sit by myself without falling over. I could hold my toys.

When I was three years old I went to Nursery. I learned to ride a trike.

When I was nearly a year old I learned to crawl everywhere!

When I was five I started school. Then I learned to climb in PE.

I came to Britain from Jamaica

One day, I got a letter.

It was from my mum and dad.

They wanted me to come to Britain.

They sent me a picture.

I came to Britain on an aeroplane.

It took all night, and I had to sleep on the plane.

Valerie Fawcett

The House at Night

Everybody needs to feel warm and safe before they go to sleep, and so does the house. The grown-ups lock the doors, draw the curtains and switch everything off. How do you prepare for sleep? Probably first of all you change into your night-clothes, brush your teeth and say goodnight. Do you have a bedtime story, a favourite toy or a night light? Are there things you like to think about, just before going to sleep?

Lights make us forget the dark outside. How do you feel when the lights go out and everything looks different?

At night other animals are quite active. Minibeasts crawl out of their hiding places and search for food. Cats like to hunt and explore but a dog is happier to sleep and dream.

Stephen Webster

ANIMAL SENSES

Animals use their senses – touch, smell, taste, sight and hearing to find out about the world around them.

Here are some amazing things that animals can do:

A DOG USES its sense of smell to find out all kinds of information. Bloodhounds can even detect the microscopic pieces of skin that are shed from a moving person's body.

A SHARK CAN smell blood in the water hundreds of metres away.

SOME SNAKES CAN feel the heat rays from animals they want to eat, like mice. They use their tongues to taste smells in the air.

CRICKETS HAVE EARS on their knees which help them to hear their mates.

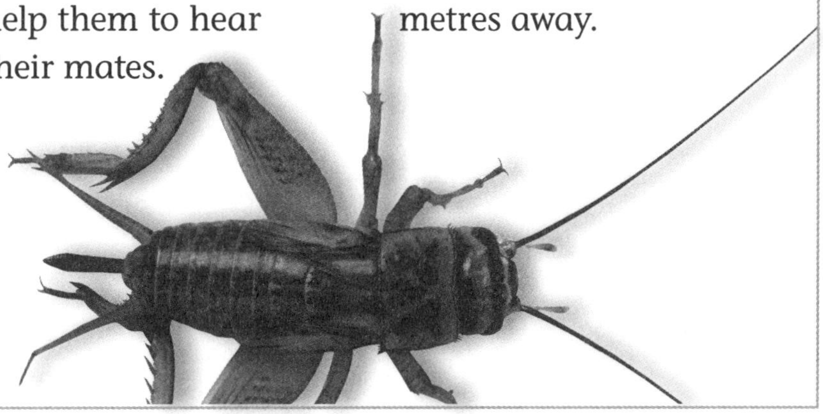

FLIES HAVE TASTE sensors on their feet, to test food when they land on it.

A FENNEC FOX'S huge ears help it to hear danger or find food to eat. The fennec fox can hear a desert beetle kicking over sand grains many metres away.

Dorling Kindersley Children's Illustrated Encyclopedia/Wendy Jolliffe

Acknowledgements

The publishers gratefully acknowledge permission to reproduce the following copyright material:

Andersen Press Ltd for an extract from *Little Red Riding Hood* retold by Tony Ross © 1978, Tony Ross (1978, Andersen Press); for an extract from *Follow My Leader!* by Emma Chichester Clark © 1999, Emma Chichester Clark (1999, Andersen Press); for an extract and illustration from *Where Are You, Blue Kangaroo?* by Emma Chichester Clark © 2000, Emma Chichester Clark (2000, Andersen Press) and for the covers from *UFO Diary* by Satoshi Kitamura © 1989, Satoshi Kitamura (1989, Andersen Press). **Belitha Press** for an extract from *Keeping Fit* by Paul Bennett © 1997, Paul Bennett (1997, Belitha Press, an imprint of Chrysalis Group plc) and for an extract from *Rain and Us* by Jillian Powell © 1998, Belitha Press Ltd (1998, Belitha Press, an imprint of Chrysalis Group plc). **Anthony Browne** for use of an extract and illustration from *Through the Magic Mirror* by Anthony Browne © 1976, AET Browne and Partners (1976, Hamish Hamilton). **Carolyn Dinan** for a new illustration for *But Martin!* by June Counsel, illustrations © 2004, Carolyn Dinan. **Faber & Faber** for 'The Frog Prince' by the Brothers Grimm retold by Stephen Corrin from *Stories for Six-year-olds* edited by Sara and Stephen Corrin © 1967, Faber & Faber (1967, Faber & Faber). **John Foster** for 'When the Wind Blows' from *Four O'clock Friday* by John Foster © 1991, John Foster (1991, Oxford University Press). **HarperCollins Publishers Ltd** for an extract and illustration from *The Tiger who came to tea* by Judith Kerr © 1968, Judith Kerr (1968, HarperCollins). **David Higham Associates** for an extract from *The Brave Little Grork* by Kathryn Cave and Nick Maland © 2002, Kathryn Cave (2002, Hodder Children's Books) and for 'There Was an Old Woman' from *Collected Poems for Children* by Charles Causley © 2000, Charles Causley (2000, Macmillan). **Hodder & Stoughton** for an extract and illustration from *Hearing* by Mandy Suhr, text © 1993, Mandy Suhr, illustration © 1993, Mike Gordon (1993, Hodder Wayland) and for illustrations from *The Brave Little Grork* by Kathryn Cave and Nick Maland, illustrations © 2002, Nick Maland (2002, Hodder Children's Books). **Julie Holder** for 'Porwigles' by Julie Holder from *The Flumps Annual* © 1978, Julie Holder (1978, World Distributors Ltd). **Jean Kenward** for 'Summer Rain' by Jean Kenward from *Secrets* compiled by Judith Nicholls © 1998, Jean Kenward (1998, Ginn). **Wes Magee** for 'Who Likes Cornflakes?' by Wes Magee from *Hop to the Sky* chosen by Brian Moses © 1999, Wes Magee (1999, Ginn). **Tony Mitton** for 'Minibeast Movements' by Tony Mitton from *Secrets* compiled by Judith Nicholls © 1998, Tony Mitton (1998, Ginn). **Oxford University Press** for an extract from *I Came to Britain from Jamaica* by Valerie Fawcett in *Fact Finders,* Unit B, *Families* © 1994, Valerie Fawcett (1994, *Oxford Reading Tree,* Oxford University Press). **Penguin Group UK** for an extract from *Baby Animals* by Angela Royston © 1992, Dorling Kindersley Ltd (1992, Dorling Kindersley) and extracts from 'Animal senses' from *Children's Illustrated Encyclopedia* © 1991, Dorling Kindersley Ltd (1991, Dorling Kindersley). **The Random House Group Ltd** for an extract from *But Martin!* by June Counsel, text © 1984, June Counsel (1984, Faber & Faber), new edition to be published in 2005, Doubleday, used by permission of Transworld Publishers, a division of The Random House Group Ltd; for an extract from *What's in Your Pocket, Lucy Locket?* by Paul and Emma Rogers © 2000, Paul and Emma Rogers (2000, Bodley Head); for an extract from *Inside My House* by Stephen Webster © 1994, Stephen Webster (1994, Bodley Head); for an extract from *What Can I Write? Rosie Writes Again* by Martina Selway © 1997, Martina Selway (1997, Hutchinson); for an extract from *Falling Angels* by Colin Thompson © 2001, Colin Thompson (2001, Hutchinson) and for an extract from *Tell Me What It's Like to Be Big* by Joyce Dunbar © 2001, Joyce Dunbar (2001, Doubleday) used by permission of Transworld Publishers, a division of The Random House Group Ltd. **Marian Reiner Literary Agency** for 'Weather' from *Catch a Little Rhyme* by Eve Merriam © 1966, Eve Merriam (1966, Macmillan). **The Salariya Book Company** for extracts from *From Seed to Sunflower* by Dr Gerald Legg © 1997, Dr Gerald Legg (1997, The Salariya Book Company). **Marian Swinger** for 'The Three Little Pigs' from *The Works* chosen by Paul Cookson © 2000, Marian Swinger (2000, Macmillan). **Barbara Taylor** for an extract from *Insects and Other Minibeasts* by Barbara Taylor © 2002, Barbara Taylor (2002, Oxford University Press). **Charles Thomson** for 'Whose is it?' from *Another First Poetry Book* compiled by John Foster © 1988, Charles Thomson (1988, Oxford University Press). **Walker Books** for an extract from *It's the Bear!* by Jez Alborough © 1994, Jez Alborough (1994, Walker Books) and for an extract from *When I'm Big* by Debi Gliori © 1992, Debi Gliori (1992, Walker Books). **The Watts Publishing Group** for an extract from *Lucy's Picture* by Nicola Moon © 1994, Nicola Moon (1994, Orchard Books).

Every effort has been made to trace copyright holders for the works reproduced in this book, and the publishers apologise for any inadvertent omissions.